MEMORIES
ARE A REFLECTION OF
Our Past

MEMORIES
ARE A REFLECTION OF
Our Past

PAM FIECKE

CITIOFBOOKS, INC.
3736 Eubank NE Suite A1
Albuquerque, NM 87111-3579
www.citiofbooks.com
Hotline: 1 (877) 389-2759
Fax: 1 (505) 930-7244

Ordering Information:
Quantity sales. Special discounts are available on quantity purchases by corporations, associations, and others. For details, contact the publisher at the address above.

Printed in the United States of America.

ISBN-13:   Softcover   979-8-89391-975-2
                eBook   979-8-89391-976-9

Library of Congress Control Number: 2025917754

All Bible quotes taken from King James Version.

TABLE OF CONTENTS

Introduction i

In Honor And Dedication.. iii

The Beginning Of A New Year (January)

A Start Of A New Year Of Living And Learning 2

We Were Born With A Purpose In Mind 4

Standing Strong In Your Beliefs 6

Be Still 9

The Value In Heart Prints 10

Love Is In The Air (February)

Love Is Simple 13

Love Comes In All Shapes And Sizes................................15

Two Different Kinds Of Love 16

Love Is Immeasurable 18

Our Hands: Instruments Of Grace 20

Spring Brings On Signs Of Renewal (March)

Jesus Brings A Light To Our Path 23

Reminders Within Our Day 24

We All Need To Be Spiritually Nourished 27

The Source Of Light 29

The Season Of Unpredictable Weather............................32

Lessons We Achieve Everyday (April)

Children Teach Valuable Lessons 35

Carrying Out Acts Of Kindness.....................................37

Everyday We Hope 39

The Doctor Visit..40

In Our Weakness, We Find Strength................................42

Celebrating What's Close To The Heart (May)

Finding Courage And Faith...46

The Hidden Gift 48

Our American Flag...50

Mother's Live In The Hearts Of Their Children..............................52

Celebrating Amazing Mother's 54

Summer Time, Special Occasions (June)

Walk In The Light Of His Love 56

Examining Our Hand...57

A Milestone Of Achievement..59

Father's Are Special 61

Traveling Together In Unity...62

The Many Things Summer Has To Offer (July)

Freedom Is Never Free 65

Searching For A Wise Investment 67

Learning And Discovering 70

Children Are The Essence Of Love 72

Enjoying The Summer Time...75

Carrying On In A World Of Beauty (August)

Never Without Our Shepherd 79

Swapping Sandles 81

The Perfect Plan...83

Everyday We Hope 86

Cookbooks Carry On A Tradition 88

Fall Is A Beautiful Time Of The Year (September)

Fall Surrounds Us In Nature's Beauty......................................91

The Artist Is At Work..93

Our Greatest Lessons Learned...95

The Purple Crayon...97

A Hug Generates Goodwill To Others 100

A Time Of Harvest (October)

Greeting Our Day...103

In The Midst Of Seasonal Change 105

May The Bible Be Your Source, And Scripture Find You The
Answer..107

Quilts Have A Story To Tell 109

Your Not Only A Magnet In My Life, You're A Treasure 111

Giving Thanks (November)

In Everything Give Thanks 115

A Grateful Heart..117

Colors Of Faith..119

The Tree House..122

Do This In Remembrance Of Me 124

For Unto Us A Savior Was Born (December)

The Greatest Gift 127

The Light Of The World..129

The Candy Cane Is Special..131

God Sent Us A Savior 133

Sending A Message Of Love, Hope, And Cheer.......................135

About The Author..**139**

About The Author..**140**

About The Author..**141**

About The Author..**142**

About The Author..**143**

About The Author..**144**

About The Author......................................145

About The Author......................................146

About The Author......................................147

About the Author......................................148

About the Author......................................149

My Autobiography......................................150

Introduction

Everyday is a blessing from God, we, just never know how that day is going to go for us.

We, can have a strategy to plan our day, think about our day, visualize what might happen within our day, but in all reality, God is in charge!

There will be people coming and going in and out of your life, sharing life's ambitions with you.

You will learn, that there are know two days that are identical to each other, everyday is a completely different day with things to do, people to see and places to go.

In all that you do in your day, make it a learning experience that touches your heart and soul, not only for yourself but, with the people you are with as well!

Always find time to laugh, giggle, tell stories, run, jump, sit in silence and reflect on your memories of your past!

Let all that you do become a lasting memory you can relive and share down the road with others in a positive manner too!

My first book with a Platinum Seal and is world — wide is called, "Inspirational Stories that Spark our emotions and Touch the Heart and Soul." and now, I welcome my next edition, "Memories are a Reflection of our Past!"

In each of these books you will read a host of Inspirational Stories, written in creativity, that will arouse your curiosity, will educate, encourage, and will touch your heart and soul in a meaningful way!

Let everyday nurture and consume your inner most well being in a resourceful way. Let your imagination expand and bring on a day that the out-come is the best in all that you do!

We, are to live as an example of Jesus and to lead the way, step by step and to light the path for others.

Let our words, our peace, our reflection, of beauty come alive in a most positive way to bring happiness to those near and at afar!

In Honor And Dedication

In my lifetime, there have been many people who have helped me, cared for me and shaped me into the person that I am today. They have brought happiness to my day and simply left an inspiring mark on my heart and soul, that never subsides or leaves me.

They have given me good direction and guided me into success in a healthy way of living. They encouraged me to go on and be the best I could be with my God-given talents.

I, would like to acknowledge my family, friends, neighbors, teachers, and the surrounding communities for all they have done to help me along life's journey.

A special Thank You to: My agent - Chloe Bennett, Citi of Books of Albuquerque, NM and all of their wonder qualified staff for all they have done to promote, and venture into new horizons with my Inspirational Books!

Citi of Books gave me wonderful direction, a positive outlook and guidance to all of my many questions and concerns. Citi of Books made me feel comfortable and confident at all times when talking to them. We, were very proactive working together through-out the Inspirational Books.

We, all worked together in harmony to achieve success, with the first edition, "Inspirational Stories that Spark our Emotions and Touch the Heart and Soul," in a short time receiving the Platinum Seal, I, now "Welcome" the second edition, "Memories are a Reflection of your

Past" coming into the world around us for you to read and enjoy all the heart felt stories!

A Special Honored And Dedication Tribute To The following:

These three individuals have been a contribution to my writing success in different areas of my writing adventure. They helped me along the way in different ways to bring forth my God given talents to share with the world around us!

Dan Birkholz: (Herald Journal Digital & Production Manager) Years ago Dan taught me how to Blog my Stories!

Blake Shelton: (American Singer, Song Writer & Television Personality) Blake and I combined together as a team! I, am the lyricist for the songs and he sings with his band the songs I created, in a beautiful way with his talents to share with the world around us!

Austin Neaton: (Winsted Herald Journal Staff Writer/Sports) Austin is a wonderful article story writer for the Herald Journal and will be contributing his time to writing the story behind all the determination, exhaustion, tenacity, and the on-going journey of my five writing skills that has gone world-wide, followed by success!

I, Thank everyone, for all they did in anyway to help me master my writing skills into something to share with the world around me and to help those in need of hope within their day!

THE BEGINNING OF A NEW YEAR

(JANUARY)

A Start Of A New Year Of Living And Learning

We're at the beginning of a new year again. What will this year bring?

Most of us close our eyes, exhale, and give that big sigh in wonder.

Being in a economy crisis, it's hard to tell. It feels like we're on a roller coaster going up and down, taking sharp curves and having abrupt sudden stops. I'm sure we can all relate and hesitate when buying any type of large investment.

From day-to-day we may juggle ideas in our mind, give an opinion, or suggest to others how to build that better world.

The point of the matter is, we're all in this together, no matter how we look at it. Everything affects everything within our surroundings.

We need to find that avenue where we can keep a positive attitude while were trying to stay afloat in our rickety-rackety uncertain days. We also need to trust in our maker from up above, he's in total control.

Some may find it necessary to revise their night-out activities to a simple game of cards with friends, or perhaps a board game surrounded by a bowl of popcorn and a cup of hot chocolate or cider.

For some of us, years ago, this was our fun for the evening.

Extravagant ways aren't always the answer for fulfilling our needs from within.

We all have to be patient and wait it out, for in time, things change for the better, hopefully.

Some may think of the economic crises as God's plan of remodeling, redoing, restructuring, revising, revamping, reminding... us to live within our means; to help others or to lend a helping hand in time of need.

What we do for others, from within, will determine the size of our hearts and the love we have for mankind.

A perfect example will always shine on the occupation of a nurse or any kind of medically-trained person. If you've ever met a person in this profession that went beyond the call of duty, you met an angel. They are a godsend!

These people have a God-shaped way of caring, giving of themselves, nurturing, and meeting those special needs.

They never walk away from a difficult situation. They find the avenue of touching the inner core of the hurt, and the heart and the soul of any human being of any age. They're people on a mission to make the world a better place for mankind.

They have their compass needle focused 24 hours a day in a realistic manner, shining through out the world in a much needed plan of action.

Matthew 5:14 16: "You are the light of the world. A city set on a hill cannot be hidden. Men do not light a lamp and then put it under a bushel basket. They set it on a stand where it gives light to all in the house. In the same way, your light must shine before men so that they may see goodness in your acts and give praise to your heavenly Father."

We Were Born With A Purpose In Mind

There have been many interesting stories about how babies have been born into the world. This includes how, when, where, and what happened? We, all question our existence into the world.

Myself, being born a little over 4 pounds, with a head of dark, thick hair going in all directions — I mean in all directions! I laugh everytime I see a picture of me being held in the arms of someone, and I see my hair absolutely out of control!

You would never know it today, as it's usually neatly styled.

Maybe, I was the one they saw years ago and then they came up with the phrase, "You having a bad hair day?"

Besides all of that, I was very pretty and loveable baby once they got my hair under control. I had to fight a little being there wasn't much poundage there, to make it in life, as technology wasn't what we have today.

Because I was so small, they called me their little "peanut" I'm sure those around me were whispering sweet secrets in my ear, trying every which way to get me to extend that beautiful smile of mine, comparing my hands to theirs, and looking at the size of my feet.

These are the same things we still see today with babies of any size.

Then they told me they put me in a shoebox to see of I would fit. Being so small I fit perfectly in the shoebox.

Today, I smile, exhale, and roll my eyes at what they did with tiny, little ole me!

In return, I always come back to them with humor and say, "At least you didn't put the cover on the shoe box."

When seeing a shoebox today, I am amazed at how small I actually was.

This is a good illustration of how small babies were back then, and how they still made it in the world. There are today, babies that are under two pounds who survive, due to the updated technology they have today.

The shoebox story is just a fun little memory of my past.

However, on the reality side of the shoebox story, there are people who do put the cover on the box in today's world; we call it "abortion." These people don't understand that before we were born, God knew we were to be! Every life is significant to Him, for He died for that life.

This verse alone should tell us how important we were in His plans; "Truly, you have formed my inmost being: you knit me in my mother's womb. I gave you thanks that I am fearfully, wonderfully made; wonderful are your works. My soul also knew full-well; nor was my fame unknown to you. When I was made in secret, when I was fashioned in the depths of the earth. Your eyes have seen my actions; in your book they are well written; my days were limited before one of them existed." *-Psalms 139: 13-16*

We, were called, we were named, we were claimed, even before we were born. That's a wonderous thought, awesome gift from God; given unto us, in His own image. We came into the world with a purpose in mind.

Standing Strong In Your Beliefs

Dedicated in Honor
To: (Austin Neaton of MN)
Winsted - Herald Journal
Staff Writer/Sports

As we start the beginning of the new year, we are all looking for new ways to upgrade somewhere within our life.

We may even question ourselves, what needs a little bit more focus or attention within our day or perhaps our lifestyle?

Some people come up with great ideas everyday, but they never follow through. There was nothing gained because the person was lacking courage, confidence or had no goal in place for himself/herself.

Sometimes, we may even be a little hesitant in selling a product, goods, or service.

Myself, having a background in business and formerly being a consultant, was taught to dip down deep into our own inner soul, and trained, you, yourself, have to be sold first, before you can do the selling job.

In reality we have to believe in the product or specific thing before we are ready to stand for it. You then have been properly trained!

Then, to take that knowledge and apply what you were trained into full practice into the world around you.

The training must be focused on ethics and value in order to succeed. Most people want to be honest in the business world and want to establish a reputable job in sales and service.

If you really think about it, we all serve and serve one another somehow or someway everyday. One real strength is found in our own convictions. Our convictions can also be stronger than our fears.

Conviction refuses to court popularity, it defies opinion.

A good example of the word conviction from the Bible, to me, would be the story of David and Goliath. David stood before Goliath without a sword and defeated Goliath! David believed and he had an inner conviction to stand for what he believed and he stood strong and won!

Most often you will hear someone say or use the word committed.

There is a huge difference between those two words. Anyone can be committed to something. That doesn't always mean you are enjoying or believing in what you are doing.

You are technically making a promise, doing your part in whatever you agreed upon, then going through the motions.

The biggest question is, "Did you just believe in what you just did, bought, or said?"

The real element in life is understanding that we all need to believe in something, before we can truly stand for it. We, need to be committed, and then take that commitment one more step beyond ourselves to bring out the best of our true inner self.

If, you have a strong conviction in what you are doing, those feelings will be transferred to others, that what you are doing is honestly right.

When we have the courage and confidence to share our inner convictions and visions with others, our fellow men will see and feel, no matter the price they have to pay, they will be moved from within that right is being done.

They will also stand strong, along with you, in that commitment because of the conviction that was transferred to them from you.

May we all have conviction from within, that we can share with others, that's of value to mankind.

Something each of us can say, "I strongly believe in..."

In the center of our soul is the place where God dwells, and where, if we enter and close out every other sound, He will speak to us.

It's not the college or academy, but in the silence of the soul, that we learn the greater lessons of life.

Take the time to find the stillness within your day. You will then realize you have met peace from within yourself, as well.

Be Still

As, we are crossing the threshold of a new year, it is an opportunity to reevaluate our lives in the light of the future.

Anyway you look at it, we are living in a technological age geared to speed.

In the hustle and bustle of today's living, who has time to be still?

Sometimes a 24-hour day is insufficient time to complete all we have scheduled on our calendars.

We are always in a hurry, rushing from one thing to another.

We keep the radio, stereo, and television on because we cannot stand the stillness.

We rush through the fast food, driving through lines with a cell phone in one hand and money to pay for our food in the other. It is, as if, we are on a carousel revolving so rapidly we cannot get off.

We remember something we have forgotten to do. The phone rings. The noise of the world about us becomes louder and louder.

Yet, times of quiet are necessary for our spiritual well-being.

The world says, "Be active, be busy, be industrious."

But God says, "Be still," be quiet, don't rush. There are times we have to learn to, "Be still!"

The Value In Heart Prints

As we are into the beginning of the new year, there are some who choose to take the time to write down a new year's resolution for themselves.

In most cases, this involves the person wanting to make a change in their lifestyle or within themselves, to better something around them, or to try and achieve some type of a goal. It's the first step, wanting an uplift on behalf of the human side of ourselves.

As we were all handed a mirror and asked to look into it, we should be face-to-face with ourselves. This may seem like an unusual thing to do, but it would give us the opportunity to visualize that we are a reflection of God.

As we were asked then to put our hand on the mirror, we should leave fingerprints. Whatever our hands touch, we have fingerprints — on the walls, on the furniture, the TV screen, doorknobs, dishes, books, microwave, stove, etc. as we touch we leave our identity.

As we were asked to give something beautiful to another person, there would be so many material things that we could give to them to see and touch. We sometimes think that the greatest and the biggest things are the real answers to true happiness in life. Unfortunately, they're not.

It's the simplest and smallest things we do, with "great love," that brings happiness to another person. Of love, of listening.

In the eyes of all humanity, life takes on a better meaning when we leave behind "heart prints" Heart prints are acts of compassion, of understanding, of love, of listening, of caring, and of kindness.

"The best and most beautiful things in the world cannot be seen or even touched, they must be felt with the heart!"

Heart prints are good actions forwarded onto another person and then nestled within their heart, bringing them joy, peace, happiness, and an outpouring of love that spreads from one another.

We are all God's extension cords, taking our light to the day and empty places of our world, bringing an added touch of brightness for all the world to see.

Love Is In The Air

(February)

Love Is Simple

February is Valentines month, a special time for sharing our love to family, friends, and those who touch our heart in a special way.

It's a time when we should recognize the importance of the word "love."

One of our basic needs is to be loved, to have someone who cares for us. It's been said that "love" cannot be defined, it has to be demonstrated, it has to be experienced.

God has given us the greatest demonstration of the word, "love." He died on the cross for our sins. He performed a job no other man could do in his place.

Some people look for "love," some people try to understand "love," some people dream about "love," some people chase after "love," some people find "love" and some people don't.

One thing about "love," is that it never changes. It remains constant and available in unlimited supply.

"Love" is respectful, honorable, noble, and honest. "Love" is gentle, compassionate, willing to share and able to comfort at any given moment.

You know that "love" is present when in the midst of a storm, you can find even one thing to laugh about, smile about, and hold onto!

You may only be the only expression of "love" that another person comes in contact with on any given day!

"Love" comes in all shapes and sizes. "Love" is simple. In time, we'll understand that "love" harmonizes with all things and all people. "Love" is the greatest gift of all.

Love Comes In All Shapes And Sizes

Valentines Day has always been known to be considered the month of love.

The love we are talking about is often hard to describe. It comes in all shapes and sizes and all ages of mankind.

There is no job description, sales tax, dress code, time clock, expiration date, refrigeration, permit, batteries, registration, identification cards, or strings attached.

Love is simple. It is the experience of joy. The voice of love is always calling out to you!

Love offers you everything you need and desire.

Love wants to hold you, comfort and lift you. Love knows you! It knows what you have to offer life. Love will not leave you, dishonor you. Love will not rush you.

Love is ready and available at all times and in all circumstances. Love understands what the eyes can't see or the voice can't speak.

Love is a natural instinct. Love makes us feel totally accepted and totally fulfilled! Love feels good because, it is good for the heart, mind, and soul.

We are all naturally a product of love, and the greatest love ever known is God's love!

Two Different Kinds Of Love

There has never been, and never will be, a child that is born into the world that will have been conceived unnoticed!

God knew you well in advance, and has a special plan for you.

Jeremiah 1:5 "Before I formed you in the womb, I knew you. Before you were born, I set you apart. I appointed you as a prophet to the nation."

There once were two women who had different ideas for the word "love" and the "love" of life. The two women never knew each other.

One you do not know or remember and the other one you call mother. Two different individuals shaped to make you one.

One became your guiding star, the other became your sun.

The first one gave you life, and the second one taught you how to live it.

The first mother — you grew in her tummy, the second mother you grew in her heart.

The first gave you a need for love, the second was there to give it.

One gave you nationality, the other gave you a birth name.

One gave you emotions, the other calmed your fears.

One saw your first precious smile, the other dried your tears.

One sought for you a home she could not provide, the other prayed for a child and her prayer was answered.

One said "Hello," and the other one said "Goodbye."

One taught you to pray, while the other prayed in behalf of you.

From infant to adulthood, one may wonder what you were a product of — heredity or environment. Neither.

You were brought into the world given God's grace and heartbeat that you share as one.

Everyday you become wise and strong for you learned about the two different kinds of love.

Love Is Immeasurable

Soon, it will be Valentines Day which always brings to mind that four-letter word, "love."

The word love is used in so many different ways and is the most overused word in the English language. It's a word that has been given a lot of mileage for being in the dictionary, just like any other word. But other words don't have the same effects or outcome as the word love does. Love never wears out, fades away, or leaves us.

Valentines Day is a special time set aside for showing our love to family, friends, and special people in our lives while, choosing flowers, a special card, dining out, or it can be as simple as just being with someone and sharing your affection, there are many choices.

It has been said that love cannot be defined. It has to be demonstrated. It has to be experienced. The greatest love each and everyone of us has experienced is the love of Jesus when He died for us, reconciling us to God by His death on the cross.

He offered not a lamb or a bull or a goat, but Himself to do a job no other human could do.

He had proved His love in a most amazing way. This love is personal; it includes you and me. God's love is real and genuine, "for God is love." Looking back at the cross, there lies all our sins. That's a heavy load, in an earth shattering way!

As this love overflows from us into the lives of other's, we are shedding His love abroad in our needy world. If you pause just a moment and reflect upon the word "love," this will be your findings for that four-letter word. It takes a minute of your time to like someone. It takes an hour of your time to love someone. However, when you put the word "love" into action, that person will never forget that love you demonstrated to them, for a lifetime!

When we lose someone in life, their love seems to feel immeasurable at the time, but even more immeasurable, is the love they left behind!

Would the word "love" be more easily defined if we could measure it?

To use an eye dropper, measuring spoon, measuring cup, ruler, yardstick, tape measure, scale, dump truck, swimming pool, or ocean?

Every life created by God can leave an impression on their love in the world. Love is a word that is immeasurable, it's real and comes from mankind! It's built-in character that shines from within and spreads, and is contagious when experienced!

There is not one of us that can say we can live without love.

We, can exist without love, but we cannot live without love. 1 Corinthians 13. "There are, in the end, three things that last: faith, hope, and love, and the greatest of these is love!"

Our Hands: Instruments Of Grace

What if someone were to film a documentary of your hands, or a producer were to tell your story based on the life of your hands? Looking at your hands what would each of us see?

Would you see protruding veins, cuts, scrapes, scars, chapped hands, freckles, anthric fingers, calluses, grease stains, or smooth, silky, warm-to-the-touch hands?

As with all of us, the film would begin with an infant's fist, then a close-up of a tiny hand wrapped around mommy's finger, followed by holding onto a couch or chair as you learned to walk.

If you were to show the documentary to your friends, you'd be proud of certain moments, your hands held your first stuffed teddy bear, or your favorite blanket.

You took a #2 pencil and drew around your hand to make that first turkey for Thanksgiving, or a handmade valentine to give to someone special.

You learned to count to 10 extending each finger up.

Latter on, your hands extending with a gift, planting flowers, placing a ring on another's finger, embracing another person in need, doctoring a wound, preparing a meal, fixing a toy, hand shaking, placing your hand on your heart, serving others and then humbly folded in prayer.

By managing our hands they become instruments of grace-not just tools, in the hands of God.

As each of us look down at our hands they can resemble, in time, in one's lifetime, God's very hands.

Spring Brings On Signs Of Renewal
(March)

Jesus Brings A Light To Our Path

In the darkened world that we live in, it's very eye catching and soothing to the heart and soul when seeing the picture of Jesus knocking at the door.

It's early morning scene. Jesus holds a lantern in His hands representing the light of salvation.

He's willing to bring light to the darkened room behind the closed door.

One amazing thing to visually see is that there is no outside doorknob or latch. It can only be opened from the inside.

The many different kinds of weeds that are growing tall and surrounding the door bear evidence to the fact that this door has not been opened before.

Jesus is patient with us. He doesn't force himself upon us or His way into our lives. He holds the lantern in one hand and gently knocks with the other hand... .and patiently waits.

"Behold I stand at the door and knock. If anyone opens I will come in." Rev. 3:20

He has humbly brought a light for our path to walk on and for our eternity. He is always waiting for an invitation to join us in fellowship.

May the door of our heart always be open and His presence brighten our day fill us with His love and many blessing.

Reminders Within Our Day

March has been known to many as being the month of weather transition. Our weather somewhat resembles a yo-yo on a daily basis.

One day it's snowing, then it's icy with blowing snow, then it's cold, then it's raining, then the sun comes out to melt all that was poured down upon us.

Some may question, "will it go out like a lion or like a lamb?" Back and forth the weather goes. Daylight savings time begins, time to reset the clocks.

We, may become a little distressed by all the weather and time changes. We, keep telling ourselves, "In a few more months summer will be back, the weather will be warmer and the grass will be green. These little talks, thoughts, and reminders we have ourself, keeps our attitude afloat while we wait for better weather to come.

Then we may question, "what happens after summer comes?" "What keeps our attitude afloat on our not-so good days?" We, may ponder over that question.

There once was a lady who had her own idea of maintaining a good attitude, making herself beautiful and pleasing to those around her.

Everyday she looked into the mirror and thought, "what can I do to make the outside of me look beautiful?"

She had a shelf in her own personal bathroom filled with many beauty products.

She had within her everyday reach mascara, eye liner, eye shadow, and lip sticks of many shades and colors, a finger nail clippers, file, and polish of many shades and colors, shampoo, conditioner, combs and brushes, hair dryer, curlers, and curling Iron, powders, lotions, cleansing products, and perfumes in assortment of smells.

She dressed in fashion. Yes, she looked beautiful on the outside daily.

On another wall, she had an idea of what she wanted to do to make herself feel beautiful on the inside.

Her reminders weren't posted notes of what time and what place she needed to be, a grocery list, hair appointment, shopping, automotive needs, or even a beautiful picture.

She had paper clippings of reminders of how to maintain a healthy attitude, while becoming a better person on the inside on a daily basis to others, to be that pleasant person, how to control her actions, speak well of others, walk away from gossip, to be respectful, lend encouragement, and uplift others around her.

She asked for help, not from others but, from God himself, to make her a pleasant person to be around, an inspiration, and example. Another clipping said, "To live for the day, not for the past or for the future. To live for that specific day and be and do all she could do in each moment in the tick of the hands of the clock."

Another clipping said, "That she be herself, the person God intended her to be. To walk away from dishonesty, but to stand in honesty. To uncover lies and speak the truth. To not become less of a person but, to be a whole person."

Most would agree when she looked in the mirror, she had the face of Jesus. When she shut the bathroom light off to go about her day, she lived her reminders. She became that great role model and example to others daily... she succeeded!

We All Need To Be Spiritually Nourished

Somewhere within our lifetime, we will have experienced where we have been so hungry that our stomach growled and others heard it. We were also very thirsty that our lips cracked and our throat felt like a desert sand. All we could do is think about wanting a drop of cool water or one small bite of bread.

The kind of desperate longing comes when we lack something essential to life itself. The human body can go for weeks without food. It can go for days without water.

However, at some point, the body cries out for what it must have to survive. We all need to be nourished in some manner.

Without food or water, we wither up and die. In the same way, we need spiritual food and drink bread and wine for our soul.

If, we go without these things, we become spiritually malnourished! Our faith seems dry. Our prayer life seems empty. Our joy begins to wane. We are on the verge of spiritual starvation.

When we nourish something, we feed it, provide it with things needed for life and growth. To nourish means to keep up, make grow, foster, promote. Fair treatment nourishes good will. To feed, means we can eat and eat. Yes, we become full, but we're still uneasy, discontent, still lacking the essential need for ourselves!

We, take a look at our body. It needs to be nourished for supply of energy. Muscle, growth etc. and anything else to make us functional human beings.

When you really come down to the true source of what needs to be nourished, we maybe peddling our bicycle backwards and not knowing it. We, may have forgotten or have not been taught in life that our soul is the most important part of each and everyone of us and needs continual nourishment at all times!

We, all need spiritual nourishment to maintain, and bread and water to live on a daily basis.

If, you really think about it, it's like, we, all need booster cables, something that is linked to us, to give us that lift in life! Our soul, energizes us, gives us strength, anchors our soul, shields, and grounds us from destruction of the evil and its ways.

In today's world, we have so many resources to turn too, it's just a matter of us wanting to nourish our soul and maintain it properly.

The amazing part is, once you are spiritually nourished, you'll want more of it. In time, you will realize you can't seem to get enough of it, and it's contagious!

The Source Of Light

It all started in a religion class when the students had a question about daylight savings time.

The discussion turned to talking about light itself. The religion teacher then asked the students to do an at-home individual class experiment, and to document their finding and report to the class how their experiment tested out for them.

Betsey came into the living room, crying and frustrated that her religion experiment failed! She had tried to carry some light from the hallway into her dark bedroom. Betsey realized that no matter how tightly she closed her hands, by the time she opened her hands, she found nothing but darkness!

Betsey was very young and couldn't understand. Her mother came and explained that light couldn't be carried that way but light could move around if you carried the source of it.

Her mother gave her two examples of the source of light. She handed Betsey a flashlight and plugged in a lamp.

Betsey could now keep the source with her without being in darkness! There are people who go off into the darkness of the world carrying the light of Christianity in their own hands.

They work very hard at compassion and self-sacrifice with people. They try to get people to love their neighbor without knowing about or loving God. Their hands open freely, but the "light" has disappeared!

You can fill empty stomachs with food, but still leave people hungry in spirit!

Some people believe it doesn't matter what you believe, it's the way you live. We need to be continually nourished by the Word of God through our Bible, churches, and religious programs, in mind and body, and soul in order to maintain.

We, have had Christianity for so long we, often forget where the light comes from. Our soul is the most important part of us in need of specific nourishment!

We, sometimes take light for granted, within time we find shadows of darkness.

At times, we may find ourselves surrounded in trouble. Unfortunately, trouble comes from many sources, sometimes from our enemies, and sometimes from ourselves. We may at times stumble and fall because of our sinful nature. The greatest lesson we can learn is that regardless how we ended up in our peculiar mess, Jesus strong arms are there to help us up again!

When we sit in darkness and turmoil, Jesus will be our light.

Jesus never promised our life would be easy. He did promise to each and everyone of us that He would be there for us in good times and in bad times.

Jesus will support us and lead us back into the light. Jesus is our strength and power.

We can't carry the light and shed the light unless we got it from its source!

We, can't have Christianity without Christ. You and I can't rid the earth of darkness, no matter what good works we do.

Only Christ, the true light of the world, can do that.

We, can carry Christ, the light in our hearts and minds and our wills. He shines through us!

Just like Betsy, we cannot carry the light in our own hands. We need to know Christ and shine through Him to bring the best of Christianity into the world around us!

Then Jesus said again unto them, "I am the light of the world, he that follows me shall not walk in darkness, but shall have the light of life." John 8:12

The Season Of Unpredictable Weather

Most of us make a daily routine every morning to look out the window and see what the weather is going to be like for the start-up of our day.

The weather we have had for the past couple of months has been unpredictable. They call it, "Minnesota Weather!" We've had roaring winds, a spray of sleet, snow, and dangerous slippery ice.

Thinking back to our childhood, most of us remember different types of winter weather and storms, somewhat like what we are experiencing today.

Some mornings begin with the soft rays of the sun warming the bed covers. Then, there are mornings where we grasp at the dazzling white landscape. The tree limbs are weighted down by the frosty iced branches. This is beautiful to see!

Years ago, it wouldn't be anything out of the ordinary to be snuggled under a homemade quilt, shivering while listening to the creaking branches outside the bedroom window.

The moaning winds made a person feel lonesome. With a big exhale and in great wonder, we pause and question, "Is morning ever going to come?"

"Yes," but with a different picture. It's somewhat like an artist who begins with that first stroke with the brush on his canvas bringing an amazing outcome to his picture!

We have had mornings where our soul may feel windblown, raw, and exposed. We feel like we're tossed into a blistery tempest with everything breaking loose.

This is only temporary, for it's been said, "The God who brings beauty out of the blizzard promises to bring peace to all after the storm."

Always cling to His promise of peace. Let Him cover your fear with His love, like a blanket of snow, soft and gentle.

Lessons We Achieve Everyday
(April)

Children Teach Valuable Lessons

"Teacher." If you define that word, you will be amazed to find that we are all teachers in life.

We all teach something to someone everyday regardless of our age or our occupation.

Never the less, little children are the best teachers in the world. They begin teaching at such a young age. They teach young women to be mothers and young men how to be fathers.

They become so skilled at it, they don't stop there, for then they teach older men and women how to be grandparents.

They teach mom's to be cooks, house cleaners, to focus their attention in all directions, to be nurses, and to be compassionate.

They teach dads to be protectors, mechanics, and to be strong for their families. They teach brothers and sisters how to share toys, rooms, and their favorite treats.

Children teach the world how to love, hug, laugh, and embrace. They teach us to look past a person's skin color and to focus on the heart. They teach us how to look beyond another one's faults, to keep peace and to respectfully go forward.

Children keep us honest and to keep our promise because they never forget the ones we made to them.

They even teach us to be scientists and professors by asking continuously "why?" - "how come?" – "where?" – "when?" and "who?" and about anything that moves or many things that don't.

Children teach adults to be silly, to be imaginative, and to look beyond the spilled milk or chocolate covered hands and face.

They teach us to have patience as their little feet can travel only so fast and their hands can only reach so high.

Children even teach us to be photographers, to hurry and get that kodak moment.

Later on in life, our children teach us that catching small fish and a few fish are the big catch of the day for children!

Children also teach us that their infectious giggles can spread throughout a room in a short time. Anyway, you look at it, children teach us many valuable lessons in life!

Carrying Out Acts Of Kindness

Dedicated in Honor
To: (Blake Shelton of Oklahoma)
American Singer, Songwriter and Television Personality

When you carry out acts of kindness, you get a wonderful feeling inside. It is as though something inside your body responds and says, "yes, this is how I ought to feel."

Kindness is an inner desire that makes us want to do good things, even if we do not get anything in return.

Volunteers polish up the rough spots in our communities by all they do. They turn unheard of and thoughtless situations into precious treasured moments.

It is, and can be, a joy within our life to do some form or act of kindness. When we respond to this inner desire, there is kindness in everything, we think, say, want, and do.

In other words, it's like saying, "Do all the good you can, by all the means you can, in all the ways you can, in all the places you can, at all the times you can, to all the people you can, as long as ever you can."

There are many people waiting for someone just like us to come along, people who will appreciate our compassion, our unique talents. Someone will live a happier life merely because we took the time to share what we had to give.

Too often, we underestimate the power of a touch, a smile, a kind word, a listening ear, and honest compliment, or the smallest act of caring.

All of us have the potential to turn life around, it is an overwhelming thought to consider the continuous opportunities there are within our day to make our love felt.

How far you go in life depends on your being tender with the young,

compassionate with the aged, sympathetic with the starving, and tolerant of the weak and strong. Because, someday in your life, you will have been all of these. A simple message: "A candle loses none of its light by lighting another candle; neither does any act of kindness."

Everyday We Hope

We, all on an everyday basis, use the word, "hope," We, may think it subconsciously, or we may say it out loud. It's a word we use when we want the best to happen within a situation.

It seems like we're always "hoping" for something. We can "hope" all we want, but if it's not in God's will, it won't happen.

Most of us, for instance, start our day with thinking about all the things we're going to do, places we're going to go, people we're going to see, and most importantly, how we're going to do what we're going to do.

We, have a vision in our mind when we use the word "hope" for something we want, or for something we want changed.

That's when God comes into play and see's our vision of the word "hope" and does the masterpiece of His thoughts of what the word "hope" actually should be for us.

Many times, we plan things in our mind. Sometimes, they're greater that what we thought they were going to be and then there are times when things turn out much differently than we ever envisioned! That's God in control!

Just think, we have people who "hope" good things for us, and then there are people who "hope" not such good things for us! That's always an interesting thought in itself. Why? Because, God saw what was "hoped," for and why. That's what makes a difference for the word, "hope" in your daily living!

The Doctor Visit

Like most children, they hear the word, "Doctor" and they become afraid.

Maybe a shot in the arm or a wound needing attention brought an experience they found not to be delightful.

One day, a young mother brought her daughter to a scheduled Doctor's appointment.

The little girl was apprehensive while waiting for her name to be called by the nurse.

Within a short time, the nurse, with a big smile on her face, announced the little girl's name. The little girl looked at her mother with her sad, droopy brown eyes and proceeded to follow the nurse into the patient's room.

The nurse reassured the little girl that her doctor's appointment was going to be pleasant.

Within a few minutes, a tall man dressed in a white coat stood before her. Her little shoulders went down as she exhaled and gave a big sigh.

The Doctor laid some medical instruments gently on a towel. The little girl stirred to see what he was going to use on her.

She silently told herself that all of his medical supplies looked harmless to her.

As the doctor looked into her ears with his scope, he asked the little girl, "Do you think I am going to find Big Bird in here?" The little girl remained silent.

Next, the doctor took another one of his tools and looked into the girl's eyes and asked, "Do you think I'll find Elmo in here?" The little girl remained silent.

Next, the doctor took his tongue depressor and told her to open wide and say, "ah." The doctor then asked, "Do you think I'll find Cookie Monster down there?' Again, the little girl remained silent.

Then, the doctor took a rubber mallet and tapped both of the little girl's knees and asked, "Do you think your legs can run as fast as Road Runner?" She shrugged her shoulders, there was no reply.

Then, the doctor put a stethoscope on her chest. As he listened to her heartbeat, he asked, "Do you think I'll hear Winnie the Poo in here?"

The little girl put a smile on her face, and filled with excitement replied, as she pointed to her heart. "You won't find Winnie the Poo in there. Jesus is in there, and Winnie the Poo is on my t-shirt and on my purse!"

The doctor gave a big laugh and said, "Little girl, you're in tip-top shape inside, as well as outside. Here's some stickers for being such a good patient."

The little girl hopped off of the examination table and skipped out of the room with a big smile on her face!

The mother turned to the doctor and shook her head and gave a hardy laugh!

In Our Weakness, We Find Strength

One day, while in a garden center, it was most interesting to find an array of many different types of potting flowers.

The flowers were all so beautiful, it was hard to decide which ones to select for my outdoor pots. There were pink, yellow, red, violet, white, and multicolored ones. The big question was, "which ones do I do?"

Looking in another section, at a distance, a ceramic pot with a beautiful pink flower caught my attention.

On the side of the pot, it was cracked.

Looking closer, the pot was designed to look that way. Written in bold letters next to the crack on the pot was written, "I may be a cracked pot, but I'm still beautiful in many ways." I chuckled as there was a story that spread throughout the nation when these cracked pots were first designed and came into implementation within the stores.

The story may have been unrealistic, but it sent a strong message to anyone who purchased one of those cracked pots for their homes.

A water bearer in India had two large pots, each hung on the end of a pole which he carried across the back of his neck.

One of the pots was perfectly made and never leaked. The other pot had a crack in it, and by the time the water bearer reached his master's house it had leaked much of its water, and was only half full.

For a full two years, this went on daily, with the bearer delivering only one-end-and-a-half pots of water to his master's house.

Of course, the perfect pot was proud of its accomplishments. The poor cracked pot was ashamed of its own imperfections, and miserable that it was able to accomplish only half of what it had been made to do.

One day the cracked pot met up with the water bearer down by the stream. The cracked pot apologized for delivering only half of a load because of the crack on the side of the pot.

The pot felt bad because of the flaw it had. The bearer wouldn't get full value from all of his efforts.

The bearer replied, "I feel sorry for the way you feel. As we return to the master's house, I want you to notice the beautiful flowers along the path!"

Indeed, as they went up the hill, the cracked pot took notice of the sun warming the beautiful flowers on the side of the path, this cheered the cracked pot.

But at the end of the trail, the cracked pot felt bad because it had leaked out half of its load, and so again the pot apologized to the bearer for its failure.

The bearer said to the pot, "Did you notice that there were flowers only on your side of the path, but not on the other pot's side? That's because I knew about your flaw, and took advantage of it."

"I planted flower seeds on your side of the path, every day while we walked back from the stream, you watered them."

"For two years, I have been able to pick these beautiful flowers to decorate my master's table." "Without you, being just the way you are, he would not have this beauty to grace his house,"

Each of us have our own unique flaws, somewhat in resemblance to the cracked pot, if we allow it, God will use our flaws to grace his table.

In God's great economy nothing goes to waste. Don't be afraid of your flaws.

Acknowledge them, and you too, can be the cause of beauty. In our weakness, we find our strength. The "Amen" of nature is always a flower!

Celebrating What's Close To The Heart
(May)

Finding Courage And Faith

In the springtime, it's most interesting when a person comes across a bird nest up in a tree.

We may find it fascinating to watch the baby birds make their way to the edge of the nest and take a peek over to view the surroundings and the unexplored world around them.

At first the baby birds are somewhat curious, then they become uncertain and shrink back to the familiar security of the comfort of their nest. Perhaps they are unsure of the strength of their own untried wings.

Insecurity comes within the baby birds as they realize their wings are all they have to recuse them from a fatal fall. They know how weak and how unproven their little wings are.

Yet, when they are either pushed out of their nest or gather courage to launch out on their own to try that first flight, they find the air supports them when they spread their wings.

Within our lifetime, how many times have we felt insecure to take that first step into a new surroundings that lies outside our familiar nest? We may feel just like the baby birds.

Most often, we take a look at our own weakness and insecurities, and we may want to turn ourselves around and head back to where we are safe and comfortable. It's sometimes hard to comprehend that, even if we are not aware of Jesus' presence, we can rest assure that He is by our side.

In other words, we are learning what it means to use our courage and to take a leap of faith. We, are merely stretching our wings so we can grow a new adventure in life.

Jesus taught his followers, "are not two little sparrows sold for a penny? And yet not one of them will fall to the ground without your Father's leave (consent) and notice... Fear not, for you are of more value than many sparrows." Matthew 10:29-31

Peter saw Jesus walking on the sea of Galilee. He cried out, "Lord, if it's you, tell me to come to you on the water."

Jesus replied, "Come." Peter got out of the boat and walked on the water, moving toward Jesus. It was when he took his eyes off Jesus and focused on the wind that he became frightened and began to sink.

He cried out, "Lord, save me!" And, of course, Jesus did!

Jesus at once stretched out His hand and caught him.

It's been amazing to find that many people still put their courage and faith into practice in today's world.

They have found that by fixing their eyes on Jesus they didn't doubt, they didn't falter and they didn't sink. Everyday, we witness people who venture into unknown territory. They still succeed without turning themselves around because of their courage and faith... just like the baby birds.

The Hidden Gift

It has been known to mankind, that when God finished making the world, He wanted to leave behind a piece of His own divinity, a spark of His essence, a promise to man of what he could become—with effort.

It was only known that God looked for a place to hide this precious gift. He explained, what man could find too easily, would never be valued by him. This became a very valued question, and curiosity emerged from all around.

"He would have to hide this gift on one of the highest mountain peaks on earth," one said. Another said, "No, I don't think that for man as, he is an adventuresome creature, and he would soon learn to climb the highest mountain peak."

Another one softly spoke, "Maybe he'd hide this great gift in the depths of the earth?"

They all thought for a moment, and then one responded, "I think not, for man will one day discover that he can dig into the deepest part of the earth."

Another one questioned, "How about in the middle of the ocean?" The answer again became, "no, because he gave man a brain to build huge ships, and they have already crossed the mightiest ocean."

"Where then?" They all turned to one another in question.

A gentleman, overhearing the conversation, slowly walked over to the crowd. He removed his hat and set it aside.

His head slowly went to a downward, reverent position. He then took his right hand, placed it over his heart, and respectfully replied. "He hid the precious gift where every man and woman would be able to find it-if they looked sincerely and deeply enough. He hid the precious gift in their heart."

Our American Flag

If you ever take the time to really look around, you will see our American flag in many different places in our country.

You will see our American flag beautifully displayed at the bank, at the courthouse, at the church, at the workplaces, at the school, at the hospital, at the community parks, at the Legion, and at our homes.

When we see someone flying the flag there are three important colors, red, white, and blue. Red stands for blood, war and courage; white stands for purity; blue stands for justice and freedom.

I believe the flag is never better displayed than when a strong wind blows, the flag is fully unfurled, and all the stars and stripes are visible.

One important element to remember is that the American flag is proud and strong to stand alone by itself. The 13 stripes represent the 13 colonies, and the 50 stars represent the state of our country.

We have also been taught the proper way to fold our American flag. We are to also have a light on it when displaying it at nighttime. Try never to let the flag touch the ground or leave it out in the rain. Any American flag that is torn, ripped, faded, and in bad shape should be given to the American Legion for proper disposal. As, we see an American flag coming in our direction we should always display proper respect and stand and place our hand over our heart.

We should pause and think about those who have lost their lives trying to keep our country free. We should be grateful to those who are defending us each and every day. They are as strong as the flag itself. For the giving of themselves, to fight for our country and its freedom.

51

Mother's Live In The Hearts Of Their Children

A "mother," being one of those myself, what a multi-tasking person we need to be. We, wear many hats and specialize in many areas within a child's lifetime.

The reality is, the moment a child is born, the mother is also born. Mom, is one of the first words a child says. To a child's ear, "mother" is magic in any language.

When you are a mother, you are never really alone in thought.

A mother needs to think twice, once for herself and once for the child. Everyday a mother is challenged with strengthening her children by overcoming obstacles with understanding patience, encouraging morals and integrity. We also try to teach our children to choose anything that doesn't look like an unwise choice. We want our children to learn from life's greatest lessons.

We, are a mother of a child who reaches into their backpack and pulls out a crumpled drawing they colored for us, or the wonderful dandelions we receive from them for flowers. Our children are also good at planting sticky kisses on our face and placing little fingerprints on our glasses.

If we could, we would build our children a dream home, or change the past, present, or predict the future, but, we can't.

Every mother is like Moses. She does not enter the promise land. She prepares a world she will not see.

A mother remains the center of attention and respect for a child, for a long time. Only to touch her skirt or sleeve makes a troubled child feel better.

Even when she is no more, her image is in the child's heart.

She manages to make the child smile. Even in the lowest period of their lives, the thought of a mother sends a message encouraging the child to go on. Every teardrop is crystallized and by the thought of a mother that was close to the child.

Mothers want their children to reach out to others and at the same time, live their lives in a meaningful way.

One of the greatest messages we can leave in the mind of a child that was close to their mother, are these words, "I have one last thing I want to teach you before I leave this earth. There is nothing that can separate a child from their mother, not time, not space, not even death. The internal side of us proves this over and over, that mothers do not die, because they live in the hearts of their children!"

Celebrating Amazing Mother's

Mother's Day is a day on the calendar selected just for mom's, grandmothers, and great-grandmothers, and if you're blessed with good health, great-great-grandmothers.

On this selected day, these women are honored for being whom they are and for what they signify.

Most women would agree, that when the plan sheet was laid out when designing a woman, God would have had to go into over-time designing that all amazing woman.

First of all, we have a lap that can hold many children at one time, and amazingly, when we stand up, they disappear.

We, have to be prepared to kiss that scraped elbow or knee, and don't forget the Winnie the Poo Band-Aids, to mend that broken heart.

Then, we have to be creative to find out what's wrong and mend that broken heart.

We, were designed with two eyes, and they see most anything north, south, east, and west of us.

We, have a nose that smells anything as sweet as honey to burn hot cereal on the stove.

We, have hands that multi-task in all directions. They are gentle to the touch when wiping a tear that's ready to make a landing.

Summer Time, Special Occasions
(June)

Walk In The Light Of His Love

Early in the morning, when it was still dark, Jimmy and his dad would go fishing. Jimmy's dad would carry the flashlight so they could see the path.

As long as Jimmy stayed by his father, in the light, he will be alright. But often. He impatiently ran ahead into the dark.

During those times, Jimmy would trip, fall, or get lost until his dad would find him. Jimmy learned that he was safe walking in the light, holding his father's hand.

Jimmy's experience offers several lessons. Sometimes, we get too busy to spend time in prayer, we let go of our Heavenly Father's hand and run into darkness. We, fall, hurt ourselves, and get lost. We, tremble in the darkness until He comes looking for us.

The Heavenly Father always finds us and the light of Christ always calms us.

Through Jesus, the darkness of our sin is replaced with the light of forgiveness and grace. He is patient with us, in spite of our sinful straying. He brings us to confess our sins and to receive His forgiveness.

Then, He comforts us and takes our hand in His, so that we may walk gladly in the light of His great love.

Examining Our Hand

One beautiful sunny day a little boy was in his community park playing with his Frisbee. With one stronger throw his Frisbee unexpectedly went sailing toward an elderly man, who sat feebly on a park bench. The elderly man abruptly raised his hand and caught the Frisbee.

The little boy went running as fast as he could to the elderly man. The little boy sat down beside him, though he didn't acknowledge the boy's presence.

Finally, the little boy asked him, "Are you ok? My Frisbee didn't hurt you did it?"

"No, I'm fine. Thank You for asking." The elderly man then asked the little boy, "Have you ever looked at your hands?"

The little boy slowly opened his hands and stared down at them. He turned them over, palms up and palms down. "No, I guess I never really sat and looked at my hands."

The elderly man then asked, "As young as you are, what have you done with your hands so far in life?"

The little boy thought for a moment, his eyes sparkling with a smile on his face. "When I was a baby I used to suck on my thumb. It made me feel secure. Then my hands got strong. I, played with toys and carried my blanket around everywhere. My hands then played with tucks and building blocks. I played ball and raked leaves with my dad.

The little boy was curious, "why did you ask me that question?"

The elderly man replied, "We, should all be grateful we have our hands. My hands have served well over the years.

My hands have been tools I have used all my life to reach out and grab and embrace life. When I was a toddler my hands braced and caught me before I crashed upon the floor."

"They have put food in my mouth and clothes on my back. My hands tied my shoes, pulled on my boots, and buttoned my coat."

"My strong hands allowed me to climb trees and swing from a rope that hung in the tree. I played ball with my friends. My hands held my girlfriend's hand and both hands held her tight with love."

"My left hand soon became decorated with a wedding band that showed the world that I was married and loved someone special in life. Down the road I held my newborn in my hands. I wiped my children's tears and caught them before they fell upon the floor."

"My hands have consoled and helped neighbor's and gripped together in anger when I didn't understand life's problems. They trembled when I walked my daughter down the aisle of her wedding. As, time went on my hands shook and trembled as I wiped the tears when they buried both my parents. Over the years, my hands have been dirty, scraped, swollen, scarred, and bent. Yet, they were strong in times of need to help others."

"Now, being elderly, not much else works but my hands, which hold me up, lay me down, and again, continue to fold in prayer. These hands are a mark of where I've been and the ruggedness of my life. But more importantly, it will be the hands that God will reach out for that will lead me home. He won't care where these hands have been or how many scrapes, cuts or bruises are on them. What he will care about is whom these hands prayed for and whom we helped along life's journey."

A Milestone Of Achievement

It's that time of the year when Graduation parties are going full force, like wildfire!

Now is the moment to take the time to pause and embrace the milestone you have achieved in your life.

From Pre-school to the 12th grade, you have been surrounded by some classmates for the whole duration of the consecutive years.

There are also some friends you hold dear to your heart as you move onto many different directions to pursue higher education.

There were many teachers who were giving it their best shot daily for you. The teachers want to achieve their grand achievement as well, and that is by teaching you to retain knowledge, skills, and all the above, down the road, to what was learned went into success.

You will always remember the school or schools you attended, the classmates, the salutatorian and the valedictorian, the receiving of your diploma, the handshakes, the tassel being moved to the side, the throwing your graduation hat in the air, all the many hugs and best of luck wishes extended to you!

You will savor in your heart the memories of things you did together with your classmates and then, your own graduation party with family and friends.

A graduating student may even voice that, "It's a true relieving accomplishment in life!"

Always continue to be a success by your gratitude, reliability, enthusiasm, accountability, tenacity, nobleness, excellence of how you act, how you speak and how you pursue all that life has to offer. Then, tucked within yourself, your spirituality, this is an ongoing process; but the result is the greatest discovery you can find and that finding your purpose and will of God in which you pursue in life.

Anyway, you look at it, down the road, you will now become the teacher of what you were taught, to share with those around you. Best of luck to all the graduating seniors in the area!

Father's Are Special

Father's Day is a day set aside for honoring or remembering our father.

It's obvious that father's come in all shapes and sizes. Some are funny, some are serious, and some just go with the flow.

They are master minded when it comes to fixing our broken items, have arms that extend beyond when we need something high up, and have muscles, when we have something that's too heavy for us to carry.

They like to fish, hunt, travel, golf, play basketball, barbecue, farm, etc. and are versatile to their trade in life.

They are most often thought of as our learning post-someone to lean on in midst of fear, capsized with trouble, or those uncertainties in life.

It's amazing how some fathers can just look at their children raise their eyebrow or just stand up and they have that attention they needed to redirect that behavior to the point where they never had to say a single word.

Then, we have those fathers that just melt when you want something. They are known to be as sweet as pie, the wrapped around-the-finger type of person.

We, also have the relaxed fathers-the ones who grab a beverage, find the recliner, put those feet up, find the remote control and click on that favorite show. Then, within time, you're bound to find them snoozing.

After all is said and done, fathers are kind of neat to have hanging around!

Traveling Together In Unity

During the summer months, there's nothing more enjoyable than sitting in a lawn chair or bleachers, gathered together with friends, family, and bystanders, to take in a game of softball.

The softball team consists of many players, each having a valuable position in the game. We're all excited when the ball flies over the fence or someone makes a home run! Then, we become a little distressed when someone misses a high fly ball in the air or tries to steal a base!

The umpire may yell, "You're safe!" Everything about the game is determined upon how each player reacts to the opposing team's strategic maneuvers within each play.

Nobody is the whole team. Each is one player. But take away one player and the game is forfeited! That is why we have extra players on the bench to fill those given needs.

Nobody is the whole orchestra. Each one is a musician. But take away one musician and the symphony is incomplete!

We, have similarities to a chain. Each one is a link. But take away one link and the chain is broken.

In other words, we need each other. You need someone and someone needs you on your everyday walk.

To make this thing called "life" work, you gotta, "yes" we gotta, lean and support. Relate and respond. Give and take.

Confess and forgive. Reach and embrace. Release and rely upon.

Isolated islands we're not! There's no "I" in the word team. We, have been designed to play that important part that has been blessed upon each and everyone of us.

We, make the world a unique and special place when we travel that winding, uneven, dusty road together in unity!

The Many Things Summer Has To Offer
(July)

Freedom Is Never Free

Freedom is a great heritage of our land!

On the fourth of July, we, emphasize the importance and principles of our American Flag.

The American Flag has three important colors, Red, White, and Blue. Red — stands for the blood, war, and courage; while White stands for purity; and Blue — stands for justice and freedom for all.

The American Flag is never better displayed than when a strong wind blows the flag to its full, unfurled, and the stars and all the stripes are visible. The 50 stars and 13 stripes represent it all.

The dreams of our forefathers were built with blood and tears. Their boldness and courage meant to keep this country standing strong throughout the many years.

The word, "Freedom," gives each and every one of us the opportunity of freedom of worship, freedom of speech, freedom from want, and freedom from fear.

The bottom line is, "True freedom is found in Jesus Christ."

The country was founded by great people. They stood for what was right. They didn't ignore, or take for granted God's handiwork, or turn their heads to look the other way.

Just a stroke of liberty and a touch of His great hand has helped this country stand.

Our freedom has never been free; those with courage have protected us day and night. We, should pause a moment and think about those who have lost their lives trying to keep our country free.

We, should be grateful to those who are defending us, each and everyday. The military is as strong as the flag itself, for the giving of themselves, to fight for our country and its freedom.

Searching For A Wise Investment

One day a little boy was sitting on his bed and was eagerly shaking the coins out of his piggy bank.

Clink, clink, clink, the quarters, nickels, dimes, and pennies fell in a pile. This little boy was very excited with what he had saved over the years.

The little boy decided he wanted to buy something with his money that was fun! He put his finger into the hole of his piggy bank and was amazed to see he had a few dollar bills stashed away as well.

The little boy placed all his coins and dollars in a fruit jar.

He proudly walked up to his father and announced. "I, have all this money saved and I want to go to the store and buy something fun to do, something adventurous, something where I have to think and use my hands." The father chuckled a little but understood his son's needs.

When entering the store, the little boy raced to the games.

His eyes moved from one game box to another. He searched through all the game boxes from shelf to shelf. He was determined he was going to find something of his interest.

In time, the little boy held in his hands the treasure he wanted. It was an assemble yourself airplane kit. His eyes glistened as he saw all the step-by-step instructions on the back of the box.

He brought his fruit jar filled with money to the cash register and dumped it all out in front of the cashier.

There he said. "I found what I was searching for. This airplane is going to be fun to put together!"

The cashier counted the money piece by piece. She smiled at the little boy as she could see his little heart was just pounding with excitement. She paused and said to the little boy, "You have enough money for your airplane."

He even received a few extra coins back. The father took his son by hand and back home they went.

The little boy opened the box and dumped all the pieces onto the floor. The father pointed to all the pieces and said to his son, "These are the wings, the tail, fuselage, the nose, the propeller, and a plastic airplane pilot. Individually the pieces aren't much, but when you assemble them together the right way, they are valuable parts of the plane."

The little boy had curiosity in his mind. He questioned, "How do we get this airplane to stay together?"

The father replied, "This bottle of glue will hold your airplane together." The little boy was content.

The little boy's airplane somewhat resembled the church. The church is made up of many individual parts: people. We are those people. Like the pieces of the little boy's airplane, we are many different shapes and sizes.

We, too, have been created in many unique ways. Some of us preach, some teach, some encourage, some support, and some lift up others in faith.

Yet, the church cannot hold together without Christ. He is the glue that binds us together and keeps us faithful.

In a short time, the little boy assembled the airplane together with many hours of fun play time.

The little boy placed his airplane on his dresser and knew he had purchased something that was a wise investment.

Learning And Discovering

Some of us may remember when we were small, how we enjoyed and found it a challenge to climb as high as we possible could in a tree.

The strategy while climbing up in a tree was to prevent falling out of the tree.

Yet, being convinced we could get to the highest part of that tree, we continued in determination.

We, grabbed onto a limb and pulled with all our might, stretching and gripping our hands around the tree branches that surrounded us, only wanting to go forward.

Our feet played an important part in our ever-forward motion.

Our legs were entangled around the limb of the tree, supporting our internal fears. We, wanted to see how high we could get.

It was a true experience of going beyond our everyday natural abilities.

It was a feeling of freedom. Examining our every move as we went forward was a challenge. Should we take that next step, grasp on, and go forward? How much more will this limb support without breaking off from the tree?

We all know there are consequences when climbing trees, such as falling flat on our face, possibly injury and, "ouch that hurt!"

Climbing the tree and returning back down is just as challenging. We are much relieved when we are back down and can announce that we are at ground level and safe.

Zaccheus, the wee little man, had different intentions for climbing a tree, Jesus was surrounded by people, and since Zaccheus was a wee little man, he couldn't see Jesus. He wanted to see what Jesus was like.

Zaccheus, with much energy, ran ahead and climbed a sycamore tree which was along Jesus' route, in order to see him.

When Jesus reached the spot, he looked up and said, "Zaccheus, hurry down! I mean to stay at your house today " Zaccheus came down and welcomed him with delight. Luke 19: 1-6 NIV.

Isn't it amazing how we all have different reasons for what we do in life to fulfill our needs?

Zaccheus not only went to great length and measure to climb the sycamore tree to see Jesus, but the wee little man learned much more. He examined his way of life and chose to follow Jesus' ways.

The wee little man searched out Jesus, and he was saved by Jesus.

The wee little man discovered that Jesus saved him, for he was lost.

Children Are The Essence Of Love

It's without question or doubt that most of us love children. We love to watch their expressions, listen to their many questions, and chuckle over their many answers.

We're touched by the way they walk, their hand movements, their smile, the tears that come when something isn't quite right, or the sparkle in their eyes when something has excited them.

What a boring and dull world this would be without children!

Just think, there would be no need for lollipops, cotton candy, trucks, dolls that walk and talk, toy trains, tricycles, bat and ball, board games, swing set, or a sandbox. Amusement parks and carousels would be obsolete. Ponies would be out of work, Santa Claus and the Easter Bunny would have to retire.

Who would care if a baby robin fell out of its nest?

Infectious giggles would never be heard and "peek-a-boo" would disappear from the English language. If, there were no children, who would make grandparents smile?

Who would play pat-a-cake, and who would try to whistle with crackers in his/her mouth? Balloons would never pop, milk would rarely spill, and sticky hands from chocolate would be a thing of the past.

Then to look up to the sky, there would be no need for a kite to fly as high as the billowy clouds.

The farm animals would never go, "oink, moo, meow, ruff!" Little frilly hair pieces and necklaces would remain in the jewelry box, untouched!

The A, B, C, would never be sung, learned or written, along with 1,2,3, numbers!

We would be without the many who, what, where, when, and how come questions.

As I stop and think, this memory comes to mind, like it was yesterday. Joshua, my grandchild, at the age of 5, was playing badminton with his father, Jason, our son. Joshua would run and take a swing with his racket and would begin to bring on that hardy laugh. of his, he was having the time of his life! All of his energy was being used up trying to keep up to his father.

In time, Joshua decided it was time to do something else. He then grabbed the garden hose, ran to turn on the water, and began spraying the water in the air. Now, to him this was another avenue of fun!

After awhile, Jason noticed that the lawn was getting drenched. He walked up to Joshua and asked him kindly, "What are you doing? Turn off the water the lawn is really getting drenched!"

Jason knew that Joshua would have a really good answer as, his mother, Hiromi, always said to him, that he reminded her Curious George! He, too was always curious and into everything but, Curious George was very much loved and a great monkey!

Joshua, without hesitation, explained his thoughts of fun that he was having! "I'm spraying the water all over high in the air and waiting for the rainbow to come out!"

Jason chuckled and calmly explained to Joshua that he would have to wait until it rained. He would then show him the rainbow.

Joshua was trying to create a rainbow, a glimmer of brightness, multi-colored with hope within his day. In his little mind and world, he knew no different.

In time, Jason will show him the rainbow and all its many colors and Joshua may get lucky and see a double rainbow! All in all, life would not be the same without children! Let's face it, children are the closest thing to Heaven and the essence of life. They are a gift, they are joy and love personified.

Such a precious story and memory about Joshua, as a child, to this day, he hasn't changed any, he still likes Curious George, LOL!

I, told him Curious George was curious but he was still loved by many!!

Enjoying The Summer Time

Summer is one of the seasons when God displays best, beautiful parks, beautiful art work, and gifts of sensory to the world around us.

The smelling, tasting, hearing, seeing, and touching, that gives us an enormous fulfillment within our day.

The sun shines brightly, surrounded by the billowy clouds, giving us a touch of warmth and gleam of brightness. The birds are chirping with one another and flying in all directions. The squirrels make hast up and down the trees, on the grass and wooded area.

Our flower gardens, flowerpots, and hanging baskets are beautifully displayed. The variety of flowers are at full bloom, and they individually give us their wonderful fragrance.

We, are attracted to their beauty, for the flowers are very eye appealing and send a message of beauty, hope, and love.

The trees and bushes are green and filled out, giving us a scent of pine and a feeling of rooted protection on a stormy day.

The ducks and swans leave a ripple on the water as they slowly flow with their little loved ones besides them.

The parks are filled with children laughing, giggling, and smiling, sliding down the slide, climbing on the monkey bars, playing ball, Frisbee, or croquet.

Many families gather together for barbeques and picnics. The aroma of the barbecued foods spread through-out the park.

The marshmallow on a stick over an open fire, we want to create that awesome chocolate, graham cracker s'more treat!

Radios are blaring, as the teens bop to their favorite tune while playing volleyball, softball, bean bag toss, lawn darts, or just finding some time to relax in a lawn chair.

The lakes are filled with people at the beach area, children are building sand castles, splashing, and having fun time in the water. The water skiers, jet skiers, and fishermen, are all being entertained in their own individual way of excitement challenge and adventure.

Weddings, baptisms, anniversaries, birthdays, and funerals take place, touching our soul in a joyous or saddened way.

Somehow our emotions are linked to one another regardless of what occasion is being held. Our heart finds a way to extend out to our loved ones, to make that day a day of remembrance.

The shopping stores extend out to you their 50 percent to 75 percent savings on clothes and summer merchandise on brightly designed posters and magazines to get your attention.

Our churches extend that "Welcome" mat to come and partake and have our soul nourished and restored. A place that's specifically designed for us to go and receive forgiveness, to become whole, and to receive the body and blood of Jesus before the foot of the cross.

The amusement parks are filled with carnival rides, variety of foods, music entertainment, face painting, merchandise selling, and many interesting animals of all shapes and sizes to see, hear, and touch.

Our American Flag stands alone, strong, displaying the red, white, and blue colors, representing freedom for all.

The fireworks burst into the sky giving us a beautiful display of assorted colors accompanied by a loud crackle.

It's amazing to see how God designed our world to include many sensory items, taste, hear, see, and touch within our day.

Memories are a Reflection of Our Past

Carrying On In A World Of Beauty
(August)

Never Without Our Shepherd

Several years ago, a few of us decided, we were going to go to a farmers auction. To me, this was just something to do, an adventure for the day.

We got there, got our bidding ticket and started to look around at all the tractor, tools, and hay wagons full of outdoor to household items.

On one of the hay wagons, we spotted a collection of figurines. There were so many to look at, pick up, and touch.

As if I needed one more figurine to dust around.

In one abrupt moment, I spotted a figurine that was hard to part with. It's like it said to me, "bid on me!"

Over and over I looked at that figurine of, "Mary had a little lamb."

From infancy, we hear of Mary's little lamb in our children's books, and cassette tapes, and see the sweet soft ones that line the shelves in the stores.

In some churches you will see a beautiful wood carving showing Jesus cradling a lamb in his arms while older sheep stand at his feet. The comforting image shows the good shepherd, who willingly lays down his life for his flock.

At that moment, there was something about that figurine that made me feel like I wanted to bid on it. It was like it was rare and one of a kind. It reminded me of many pictures and back and forth the bid went. I just kept smiling and bidding, my little heart was pounding. How much higher should I go with my bid?

After awhile, the other person looked over at me, became hesitant, and slowly gave in. I, therefore got the bid! "Yes!"

I got the figurine after all that back-and forth bidding. Since then, when driving by and seeing sheep out in the pastures, there is a true reality side to sheep. Sheep are not always sweet, soft, or cuddly like we imagine them to be.

Sheep readily wander into trouble. Their coats often are dirty and full of burrs unless, you see them at the State Fair well groomed for judging. They need a protector, to guide them and lead them out of danger.

We, humans are the same-we need someone to help us, lead us, and rescue us from danger. Our shepherd, Christ nudges us, lifts us up into His arms when we stray from his fold. He brings us out of harm's way.

He promises that He will never allow anyone to take us out of His care.

Swapping Sandles

This time of the year, there are many people of all ages who wear sandals. There are also many types of sandals we can purchase at the store.

Generally, most of us are wanting something comfortable on our feet.

One day a young man was going for a walk. He walked with a limp, and every step showed signs of pain. His face showed what the feet were feeling.

Before we criticize the limper, we should try on his sandals. It might be an education no school, college, or sermon could teach.

The faultfinder would be more tolerant of another's limp if he had to wear, for a little while, those nail-piercing sandals the other person has to wear all the time.

What a change in tone and pace, if society were to swap sandals. Faces that once smiled, would now have tears.

The human side, and the reality of Jesus wasn't any different. On His walks His feet resembled ours. They too, became sore, calloused, and dirty.

Jesus walked many dusty, winding, gravel roads. He was on a word mission. Those two simple words are still within.

All Jesus said was, "Follow me," and they believed him. So, in faith, people gave their lives to him.

Thinking about it, this would have been the birthplace of a way of life, of a reality that would change the world forever.

People responded to him in various ways. Most became intrigued by his healing and miracles. They started attaching themselves to him.

They believed, listened, obeyed, questioned, talked with, and learned from him. They saw and witnessed Jesus' great unbelievable works. They captured the miracles no other human could do.

The followers then told others. The group of followers, in time, became a crowd of followers. There was something different about this Jesus. His teachings, actions, and conversations were powerful.

Jesus walked as a human among humans. Jesus taught like no one ever had. Some of his teachings were razor sharp with truth. He cast out his words like fishing lines and permanently touched people's souls. He laid down his own net and saved the souls of many.

Eventually, a church was formed to help others follow Jesus. It was a gathering place. A place to be nourished, to be taught, and to reach out to others.

We live in a messed-up world, not one of us better than another. We're people today, still helping and serving people just like Jesus did.

In reality, Jesus humbly put his voice, hands, and feet into motion, instead of saying, "Not me!"

Leadership is a position not all can do, but it is a job most needed, to direct people into the right direction.

"Yes," Jesus led the way by saying, "Follow me," Those two simple words still live on in today's world.

Many souls have been blessed with that U-turn in life. They simply acknowledged those two little words, "Follow me," and they were redirected to a better way of living.

The Perfect Plan

One Sunday a minister decided he wanted to eliminate stagnant ways within the church. His goal and purpose were to build up, to replenish, and to excite the parishioner's minds, and he had the perfect plan.

He wanted the parishioners to think and then to apply what was said in church to their own daily lives.

When the time came the minister stood in the pulpit and began his sermon, "I am your minister, I wear many hats throughout the day. You are a parishioner, and you wear many hats throughout your day. God is our almighty God; he wears many hats throughout the day."

"We each need to obtain and fulfill our own job descriptions. My job description never once said that I should leave my parishioners to drift off in the pews or to not gain knowledge, or to leave a soul un-nourished, be it mentally, physically, or spiritually."

"That is not written anywhere. We are to strive to meet the ultimate obligation to think Christ-like, to do Christ-like, to act Christ-like, and to be Christ like."

"I have a perfect plan. I'd like everyone to be extra attentive today for the questions I have for you."

They are brought up to want thinkers today. God has given us all minds — it's time to have everyone use theirs."

My first question for you is, "what does it mean to trust completely?"

The minister paused briefly to view his parishioners, then said, "I, will explain that to you. It means to put yourself in God's hands and know that he will bring you where you need to be."

The minister then asked his second question, "what does it mean to look beyond the moment and see the future through his eyes?" The minister paused again, allowing the parish to think, before continuing, "To believe that whatever that future might be, it is absolutely the best he has to offer."

"As time passes, we need to look at the struggles and trials we have encountered. Our experiences will prove to us that they were merely opportunities for us to grow."

The minister then extended the third question, "How often have we worried and wondered, been anxious and been surrounded with trouble in a short duration of time?"

"However, you want to think about it, through it all Jesus has been there, waiting for you to be ready and willing to learn on his strength rather than your own."

"As, we journey through life may we pray that we'll discover his perfect will for our life and the rest in the assurance that his way is always the right way."

"God has the perfect job description. With fine detail he brings us to where he wants us to be in time, not our time."

"On our journey in life, we go through many trivial ups and downs, and twists and turns. Sunny days and dark dreary clouded days. For being his creation, nothing makes sense."

"We, scramble looking for answers, searching for something we can't find, answers are hazy. Our vision is blurred. Nothing is clear, we become frustrated and disappointed."

"Then, we realize in the time that God was working all along, bringing us to where he had special plans for us. After time, we are amazed to find that through it all God's way, was the ultimate best way. His ways are the best ways, as God created us for a purpose and plan."

"What other person would know his creation any better than God himself?"

Everyday We Hope

We all on an everyday basis, use the word, "hope." We may think it subconsciously, or we may say it out loud. It's a word we use when we want the best to happen within a situation.

Seems like we're always "hoping" for something. We can "hope" all we want, but if it isn't within God's will, it won't happen.

Most of us, for instance, start our day with thinking about all things we're going to do, places we're going to go, people we're going to see and most importantly, how we're going to what we're going to do.

We have a vision to our mind when we use the word "hope" for something we want, or for something we want changed. That's when God comes into play and sees our vision of the word "hope" and does the masterpiece of his thoughts of what the word "hope" actually should be for us.

Many times, we plan things in our mind. Sometimes, they're greater than what we thought they were going to be, and then there are times things turn out much differently than we ever visioned. That's God in control.

Most think, we have people who hope good things for us, and then there are people who hope not such good things for us.

That's always an interesting thought in itself. Why?

Because, God saw what was hoped for, and why. That's what makes the difference for the word, "hope" in your daily living.

Cookbooks Carry On A Tradition

One of our greatest heritages that we have passed along and shared with others, from within the home, to city, state, and even nationwide, is the priceless collection of recipes.

It's an absolute blessing when people of the church or community gather together to design, compile, share, and sell a cookbook. Every cookbook is personified, unique and carries on it's own traits.

It would be hard to imagine a home without some sort of cookbook, hiding in a drawer or on a shelf, waiting to be used. Many recipes are selected from our own personal recipe collections, some were found in our mother's or grandmother's cookbooks.

Then, we have some recipes that are filed away. Some were given to us by our friends, while others were tried and tested.

The many varieties of recipes we get to try include; beverages, appetizers, candies, bars, cookies, pies, cakes, bread, frostings, main dishes, salads, preserves, and the list goes on.

It's most interesting when an ingredient is disguised, and we can't figure out what was added to make that luscious dessert.

Sometimes we're in wonderment of what ingredients were needed to make our bread rise or bring out that savory taste in our main dish.

When it comes to making a cookbook, it's pretty standard a cookbook can be for all ages. With a little help along the way, any recipe can be mastered by our children with our help.

Most often, you can tell right away if a cookbook has been used frequently. It will have grease stains on the pages, pen markings stating the recipe was good. The pages may be marked with a posted note paper, or the cookbook may look tattered or torn in spots.

Anyway, you look at it, it's a special time of bonding when we all gather together to share the same interests and helpful hints, and feed the soul with good food. The heart of every home begins with a savory home-cooked meal that's shared with family and friends!

Fall Is A Beautiful Time Of The Year

(September)

Fall Surrounds Us In Nature's Beauty

Dedicated in Honor
To: (Dan Birkholz of MN)
Winsted Herald Journal
Digital & Production Manager

This time of the year, we're in the midst of cooler weather and changing colors of the leaves on the trees.

Some of the leaves are already crisp and making their landing.

Most of us like to inhale and absorb the fresh cool air on a fall day. The fall season sends us a message. It stimulates and excites us. It visibly shows us that we're in the midst of seasonal change.

The squirrels are busy gathering food for the long winter months ahead of them. The gardeners are busy canning or freezing, anything from vegetables to preserves. The pumpkins are hidden under the green vines ready to show off their brilliant orange color.

The camouflage hunters are out there giving their best shots at the geese and ducks.

The farmers are getting anxious to get into the fields for harvest bounty.

The flowers are slowly closing and giving us that message of seeing us next summer.

Families are going on road trips to view nature's beautiful leaves on the trees. It's amazing how color brings on that ray of beauty to our surroundings.

During the day we open our windows for a little fresh air and then, as nighttime comes, we slowly close the windows to stay warm.

Then, there will be some of us who will be waiting for that Indian summer day, to technically announce to us that we're one with summer and now are in the transition of the fall season.

Fall is a wonderful time of the year and gives us so much beauty to be thankful for.

The Artist Is At Work

It's apparent that we're in transition of heading into the season. The weather is more brisk as the coolness of a soft breeze and dampness encompasses us.

The corn fields are drying up, the trees are turning their leaves autumn colors. The birds are heading to a warmer climate, the squirrels are gathering their bounty for the winter months ahead.

The elderly are starting to wear their sweater, or coat, finding a blanket to snuggle in as comfort of warmth.

The sun will shine and will be radiant in sending heat on some of our fall days.

When looking around, we will see an artist at work painting us a beautiful picture. Every stroke with the paintbrush send a kaleidoscope of awesome fall colors.

We will be surrounded by autumn beauty for the next few weeks ahead of us. Take time to look around and enjoy God's work of art, he never fails his plan of beauty.

For the gardeners, it's time to finish collecting all the garden produce, to be canned or to be put in freezer for the winter months ahead.

The pumpkins are bright orange hidden within the vines in our garden. The pumpkins will be used shortly for carving, decorating, or pies, for the holidays ahead us.

Slowly one-by-one a leaf will descend on its way down to the ground till the tree is bare.

The hunters are getting ready to be camouflaged to hunt their favorite game of the season.

The lawn chairs, picnic tables, outdoor games, the boat, potted flowers, and anything else that was kept outdoors will be moved into storage till next summer.

Some of our summer sports will have ended for the season and will resume come next summer.

Around and around in transition we go from season to season.

God, the artist is our artist and will always be our master artist. With his paintbrush on the canvas, one stroke at a time, one day at a time, he paints that fall masterpieces for all of us.

In doing so, he smiles.

The artist sets down his paintbrush, tears off the canvas of his completed picture, and smiles. The artist starts a new picture of beauty for all of us to enjoy, in doing so, he smiles.

The artist has a plan, it's all about us looking around and seeing that message of beauty. It's all there, for all of us to enjoy from season to season.

Our Greatest Lessons Learned

It's that time of the year, when that orange spacious bus is going to be a part of our everyday scenery again.

The children are heading off to school-like any other insecure child, scared, "who am I going to know?" stomach turning with many thoughts going through their mind in different directions. In time, that will all change for the better and they will feel comfortable.

One of our greatest lessons we were taught in school was, every morning when getting up, we decided right there, what kind of a day we were going to have. Attitude is 100 percent a part of all of us every day, no matter how old you are.

A positive, motivated student will always be successful in any school setting. The more we find enjoyment within the school system, we, then become more interested in hanging around.

Latter on in life, you will be amazed by the many times in your life, that what you were taught in your school setting, will be of importance to those around you. You were once the student; you now become the teacher of what you were taught.

We are all teachers, teaching something to someone everyday.

We would always remember that, we may not always teach with words; we teach also by who we are and how we live our lives.

One of the amazing things about it is, my teachers will always consider me as their student, while I will always consider them as my teachers, no matter what each one of us does in life.

And enough, Jesus left his footprints in the sand of the seashore, but left his teachings principles in the hearts of all whom he taught. He instructed his disciples that day and to us speaks the same words, "Follow me," John 21:22

These two simple words still live on it today's word.

The Purple Crayon

Bobby was in the first grade and was very excited about all the fun things they got to do in school.

One day, Mr. Hantz, his teacher, told the class to draw an outdoor picture of something that you like to do in the summer.

A big smile came to Bobby's face. Bobby was stirred with emotion as he reached for the purple crayon, and drew a tent.

He liked the outdoors and liked to go camping with his family and friends.

Bobby took his picture, and proudly showed it to his teacher.

Mr. Hantz took one look at Bobby's picture and said that his tent wasn't realistic enough, that purple was no color for a tent, that purple was a color for people who died.

He told Bobby that his picture wasn't good enough to hang with the others.

Bobby's head dropped forward, his shoulders went down.

Tears came to both of his eyes and his little heart was crushed.

Bobby slowly walked back to his seat, counting the swish, swish, swish, of his baggy corduroy trousers.

Laying his paper on his desk, he took one more look at his picture and mumbled to himself, "My picture is good, and should be hung with the rest of the others."

Wiping a tear from his cheek, before it landed on his picture, he grabbed, in anger, the black crayon. Nightfall came to his purple tent, in the middle of the afternoon.

In the second grade, Mr. Ruhue, Bobby's teacher, said to the class, "I want you to draw a picture of anything you like to outdoors." He didn't care what. Bobby left his paper blank, and the box of crayons remained closed.

His teacher came to his desk and looked at Bobby's paper.

Bobby's heart was beating fast and he was frozen to his seat and silent.

The teacher touched Bobby's head with his big hand and in a soft voice said, "It's a picture of a snowfall. How clean, and white, and beautiful!"

Bobby looked at his teacher in amazement.

Bobby then reached for his purple crayon and in the corner he drew a sun, and put eyes and a big smile on the face of the sun.

The teacher placed both hands over his heart and exclaimed, in joy, to the rest of the classmates, "Bobby's picture has a sun with a smile on it. How did you know the sun makes people smile? You are a wonderful artist."

The teacher picked up Bobby's picture and walked to the classroom door and taped it on the door.

Bobby sat in awe.

The teacher then went to the next student and said, "You are a wonderful artist, too. You drew a pot of flowers, and look how those flowers are growing.

The teacher proceeded to tape each picture onto the classroom door, finding something positive to say to each individual artist.

Bobby realized he now liked the art class.

Bobby quickly grabbed another piece of art paper and drew the same picture over again.

He walked up to his teacher's desk, and laid it in plain view for his teacher to see. The teacher returned to his desk after he had all the student's pictures on the classroom door.

The teacher saw that Bobby had drawn another picture, identical to the one that was hanging on the classroom door.

The teacher then approached Bobby and questioned, "Bobby will you please take your favorite color crayon and write '#2' in the corner for me?"

Bobby reached for the purple crayon and wrote '#2' in the corner for his teacher.

Bobby, looking up at his teacher, asked, "Teacher why am I writing a '#2' in the corner?"

The teacher then replied, "You are writing a '#2' in the corner because that is what professional artists do! Their artwork becomes of value over the years. I now have your '#2' professional drawing and I want to frame it and hang it on my classroom wall for everyone to see. Tomorrow in class we will be learning about the steps to becoming a professional artist. Bobby, your '#2' picture will be my classroom example. Thank you in advance."

A Hug Generates Goodwill To Others

We have all been around the elderly long enough to know they all have something to share verbally when it comes to their words of wisdom.

One day, an elderly gentleman caught me off guard and stunned me with his words of wisdom.

He always wore the most beautiful smile and his blue eyes glistened. He slowly walked with his cane is his hand to get from one place to another. He was always on some type of a mission, and very interested in people and what they did on a daily basis.

One time, when seeing him at a social gathering. I extended my hand out to him to shake his hand. I was excited to see him.

His beautiful smile came into play, he said, "I don't shake hands anymore, I only give hugs." I was astounded at first, and then startled by what an amazing thing a person could say in the presence of many people.

From that day on, those words left a message that I or any other receiver could treasure for a lifetime.

One thing about a hug, it's recommended for all ages. It doesn't stop there, for a hug generates good will.

A hug relieves tension, improves blood flow, reduces stress, and helps self-esteem It's nonpolluting, absolutely no cost, non taxable, silent performance. No batteries required, no credit card or Identification needed. Extremely personal, fully returnable.

How can a person go wrong with such a perfect gift of interaction?

Both parties feel good inside, and a touch of warmth covers each other's hearts for the day.

It's a simple interaction with humans that makes us feel wanted and respected for who we are.

If you ever see two people hug each other in a "just anywhere" place, it's heart-warming experience to see between humans. It's a burst of love between people we care for, are happy for, or want to comfort.

We, all need to be connected with each other. Hugging has a high rating in today's world.

On our joyous days and on our saddened days a hug fills that space that needs human repair and tending too.

In our everyday walk, we will always see a person in need of that wrap-around hug. It's a real booster for all ages and for all walks of life.

A Time Of Harvest
(October)

Greeting Our Day

As we great the fall morning, most of us are consistently following a pattern or daily routine of what we need to do in order to get ourselves motivated for the beginning of our day.

Most of us have heard many times, to take one day at a time, and not to worry about tomorrow for tomorrow isn't here.

If we choose to live one day at a time in thought, in action, in motives, we may have questions about the day we're living in.

Did we do something in our day that was worth living? Did we do some sort of unselfish giving deed to another person?

Did we bring joy or happiness to another person? Did we convey our words with compassion or honesty?

Did we inflict pain physically, or mentally? Did we strengthen or cheer another person within our day? Did we radiate light and love as we moved through our day? Did we walk peacefully and with acceptance?

As evening falls and we're at the close of our day, what did we do to make that day worth living?

There are know two days that are the same. We all get one chance to learn and discover about our individual day.

There is no magic or illustrated book that will ever be able to show and tell any one of us how our day is going to be.

Our days are designed for us to learn, discover, and to uplift those around us, even those we do not know.

Everyone of us makes hundreds of choices everyday. Every choice we make has an impact on our lives and the lives of others.

Everyday we need to see the beauty in the world.

Accept yourself for who you are and at the same time, we should balance the need between self-acceptance and growth.

In The Midst Of Seasonal Change

This time of the year we're in the midst of cooler weather and the changing colors of the leaves on the trees.

The leaves are most often colors of orange, brown, yellow, red, and purple.

Some of the leaves are crisp and slowly making their way to the ground. The pine tree needles are green, made of nature's pine scent and never change colors. In resemblance to God's love for us, that is, "our never changing God! "

Most of us like to inhale and absorb the fresh cool air on a fall day. The sun shines bright giving us that ray of beauty, comfort and warmth from within.

The fall season sends us a message. It stimulates and excites us. It visibly shows us that we're in the midst of seasonal change.

The squirrels are busy gathering food for the winter months.

The birds are making their way to another direction of warmth.

All our vegetable bounty has been picked, canned or frozen.

The apples have been picked for sauces and pies. In time, all that remains are the branches.

The grapes have been picked and all that remains are the vines.

The crops are being harvested and soon all that will remain are the dark rustic fields.

Flowers are withering up and some are brought indoors.

People are finding storage shelters for their, skies, boats and pontoons. Our summer recreation is at a pause for a while.

We find it adventurous to carve a pumpkin or do a little outdoor decorating.

That first piece of home-made apple or pumpkin pie smothered in whipped topping sends a smile of pure enjoyment to our face.

Hot chocolate becomes a favorite to warm our innards, We start to put on layers of clothes to keep warm.

Then, at night time it's always enjoyable to snuggle in a full quilt to watch a favorite movie.

Year after year, we adapt and learn to accept the environment of seasonal change. We, still go places and do things, however, in a cozier fashion.

May The Bible Be Your Source, And Scripture Find You The Answer

It is an absolute honor to know that God is the Author of a book, known as the Bible, that is forever selling. It is a book that has never been considered outdated, nor has it been known to fail mankind!

The book, the Bible has been specially designed for all ages. If, you will take notice, all the stories compiled were never written or ever started with, "once upon a time."

For those of you who have opened up the Bible to read from it, wasn't it worth your time? Did you ever start to read and find encouragement, or a bright light within the words you read?

The Bible was designed as a book of complete truth, obedience, and a guide for all in times of need!

The words written were never meant to hurt, they are there to help, encourage, and heal your biggest wound.

Some words are written as comfort when you are hurt, worried, or frightened. You will even find w ords t hat w ill penetrate a nd s oftly blanket your heart and soul.

The Bible was, from the start, "God breathed," we must understand that God is all powerful with comfort no human can ever match.

If you take your Bible and read Genesis 2: 18, the Lord said, "It is not good for man to live alone. I will make him a suitable partner for him."

In Genesis 2: 21, It says, "so the Lord God cast a deep sleep on the man, and while he was asleep, he took out one of his ribs and closed up his flesh.

Genesis 2: 24 says, "That's why a man leaves his father and mother and clings to his wife, and the two of them become one body."

These are a few Bible scriptures written that oppose same sex marriages.

How does one speak contrary to what the Bible has said?

We, are all accountable for our vote, and for what we feel in our heart the day we actually place our vote.

We, keep in mind what is, "God breathed," and what is not.

The questions is, should the State Constitution be amended to provide that only a union of one man and one woman should be valid or recognized in each state? "Yes "

May the Bible be your source, and scripture find you the answer the day you cast your individual vote!

Quilts Have A Story To Tell

The fall season is a time when we feel comfortable when we snuggle in a homemade quilt.

The amazing part of a quilt is that, it's just old or new scrapes of perfectly good fabric, sewn together to make a blanket that provides us with warmth and comfort.

To sit around a quilting fame with a needle in your hand is an awaking experience. One needs to acknowledge the time and effort in the art of quilting.

Quilts are pieces of fabric sewn together, like moments in time. The patience and the working together is a time to connect to another person, tell stories, or just enjoy each other's company.

Quilting is a unique project that reflects our true self.

Sometimes the fabric brings a memory to our quilt, as homemade as life itself.

Every quilt has a story to tell and is made with decorative designs that brings a tear to our eyes and warmth to our heart that lasts forever.

Some quilts deliver a message of friendship and love in every word spoken.

Some quilts offer encouragement and compassion for the places in our lives that need to be wrapped in comfort.

Every stitch is done in love and handcrafted in beauty for all to admire.

The rich earth tones neutralize our thoughts, while bold colors designs bring excitement, drama, illusion, visual, and adventure to our thoughts.

Quilts are handcrafted in many designs, an art that lives on in the heart of many who receive one as a gift.

Countless people donate many hours to make something to comfort someone they'll never meet, who may be going through a difficult time. Many quilts are made to raise funds for an important cause.

Quilters often spend their time, a part of their lives, on making quilts, so that in its giving, they give part of themselves; and in receiving of a quilt, a person accepts a gift like no other.

Our lives are quilted together by the artwork of God's design. Those that sleep under a quilt, sleep under a blanket of love.

To those of you who sit with a needle in hand on a daily basis, there are meaningful words for you, "Wherever a beautiful soul has been, there is a trail of beautiful memories."

We, quilt to celebrate and commemorate, cherish, dream, hope, remember, care, and love.

A quilt has been known to have love in every stitch, made with countless hours one could never imagine.

Enjoy the fall season wrapped up in your favorite quilt, a precious treasured gift that warms the soul and sends a message of love.

Your Not Only A Magnet In My Life, You're A Treasure

Being around the elderly has always been a passion for me.

Having a Certified Certificate in the area of health care, adds joyfulness into fulfillment of what I can do to make a difference in the quality of their daily living.

Dignity and respect are top priorities for them In all aspects.

To listen to their stories always brings happiness into my day as well. The wisdom they express about their bygone yesterdays amazes me!

Then, to be of any kind of service to them is heartwarming.

To assist them a little with their walking as they struggle those small steps is of great pleasure to me. They always manage to find a smile or something meaningful to say to you.

I have many elderly folks I enjoy immensely. Everyone of them triggers me in a different way. I have one special elderly lady friend that I don't do health care with, but I find myself totally fond of her. We, both have already openly expressed how we are magnetized to each other, and we laugh about it. We, usually attend a lot of similar functions, which makes this more fun for the two of us.

The high light of seeing each other, is enjoying each other's company. We both get excited and our little heart flutters when we see each other in a crowd of people. We, both hunt each other down and connect in an excited manner. It's just plain fun!

A while ago, I gave her a religious bracelet that had been blessed. She received it as a gift when her husband passed away. She wears it all the time and makes it very clear to me and others that she's wearing it almost all the time.

I do take a peek, and sure enough, she's wearing it. She is very protective over her bracelet and wears a smile when she raises her arm in the air to show others her wonderful gift.

Sometimes, it makes we wonder, why all friendships can't be as nurturing and simple. We both care for each other in a close-knit way. We never spark an argument or say an unkind word because we value the relationship and the fun we're having being magnets to one another.

She's not only a magnet, she's a treasure for being an uplifting person. I find this so right, to write about her because, isn't it nice to know how people feel about you when you're still face-to face in a world where love should be shown to others, not jealousy, degrading, or outrage?

The relationship of being magnetized is unique and considered a gift because we let nothing come in between the special moments we share.

It's the eloquence of who she is that attracts me to her. She is a pleasant lady and I am very fond of her and fortunate to have found such a wonderful person along my path in life.

She represents an excellent role model of what an elderly person should be like. She is all God created her to be.

I just recently told her I wanted to get something or do something special for her, but I couldn't pinpoint what so, I decided I was going to share my thoughts about her. She will laugh at that statement but hold it high within her thoughts everyday!

The name is withheld, for she knows this is written especially for her, to bring happiness into her day for just being herself.

We, simply take it one visit at a time and explore what we can about each other, while having fun, laughs and giggles; yet still, remaining magnetized to each other.

Giving Thanks
(November)

In Everything Give Thanks

Thanksgiving time is a time when the words, to be thankful and giving thanks come to our minds. Although, it seems to mean something different to almost everyone.

What to be thankful for can be a wide spread of things, from our jobs, health, home, food, money, clothing, friends, and family.

However, may we be thankful for what we are all blessed with.

In today's world, we're seeing the real enjoyment from years ago withering away right in front of us, right before our very own eyes.

The porch swings, picnic tables, and hand-written letters, are slowly becoming a part of the bygone age. We don't know how to sit still, relax and enjoy; we run, run, and are on the run!

We, are now faced with the fast-food drive-through, computer games, and emails. We are never a beeper or cellular phone call away from being summoned!

The purpose of life, is not to just get things done, but more so, to connect with each other.

Passion is important, and so is compassion. Helping others was something Jesus did on a daily basis. He was constantly approached by people, but he always found time to stop what he was doing to help those in need. This is a lesson we must learn if, we, want to be anything like Jesus.

Hands are referred to numerous times in the Bible. God's hands created the heavens and the earth. Jesus laid his hands on many; lepers were healed and the blind made to see by his touch. His hands were nailed in his sacrifice on the cross for our sins, and lifted to bless his disciples before his ascent to heaven. Our hands are to carry on his work.

We, don't perform miracles, but we can lend a hand to benefit others.

God sends people to help us when we need them. Sometimes you are the person giving the help and sometimes you are the one receiving it; both roles are important. The operative word is, "person."

It's about people, not things. Knowing, more than doing. Being more than getting.

Everyday, may we all be of some sort of service somehow, or somewhere.

Search and you will find something to be thankful for and also be blessed with. To reflect upon your day, you will realize that all along, Jesus was your example. The greatest works ever begun upon this earth were planned and started by Jesus.

A Grateful Heart

"The potatoes are boiling, the gravy is simmering, and the turkey is in the oven, filling the air with the fragrance of anticipation.

The top homemade breads shine from being smothered in butter.

The pies are cooling on the rack, overflowing with the fruits of the earth.

Family and cherished friends will gather at the table shoulder-to-shoulder, to rejoice in the bounty of blessings, and lift up their hearts in thanksgiving.

As, the table is set with freshly laundered linens, sparkling Chrystal, and gleaming China, The silver shines, the candles glow, and the flowers delight us with their beauty.

Let us rejoice and praise the giver of all good! We, have so much to be thankful for!

A grandmother once asked while surrounded by her thanksgiving guests, "who would like to say the table prayer?"

It was silent for a moment as the adults stirred looking at each other until, her grandson, at the age of 5 who was hidden among the family blurted out, "I'll do it!"

'The grandmother was astounded, for she had no knowledge of him knowing any prayer. The grandmother in awe for a moment. She then became excited thinking that any type of prayer would be sufficient.

"

The grandson respectfully folded his hands, bowed his head, and began the prayer he knew. He slowly said, "Come Lord Jesus be our guest and.... and The grandmother with a soft whisper assisted him, "and let these gifts to us be blessed, amen."

It didn't matter what kind of prayer he said, - what mattered was his prayer was meaningful to him and from his little heart.

It didn't matter how slow and how long his prayer was, what mattered was his intentions were of first learning about prayer and in time would become better at it!

It didn't matter what type of words he used for the prayer he said, what mattered was, he asked for our creator to be present, to our guests, and for our gifts, to be blessed.

It didn't matter his age, what mattered was his heart was open to giving thanks to all he was surrounded with.

We, have been blessed and surrounded with so much, that we often forget the gift of the grateful hearts. Hearts that will not forget what our creator has done for each and everyone of us.

Colors Of Faith

Jimmy one of my special little friends, recently received some clothes, activity book, coloring book, and a box of crayons, as a Birthday gift.

Jimmy's attention immediately focused on the deluxe box of more than seventy color crayons, and he was proud.

As time went on, whenever he found an audience, he would empty every crayon out of the box, then separate the color families, displaying the beauty of each color.

Once, when the process ended, he surprised a viewer by reaching for one special crayon, the periwinkle blue, and holding it high and said, "And this one is so pretty. It reminds me of my mothers beautiful eyes."

Young as he was, he knew the difference between grief, and the openness to beauty that touched his soul in a magical way, bringing warmth in his heart and a smile to his face.

Putting all his crayons back in the box, in their own special place, he turned and looked at me and asked in a spirited voice. "What is your favorite color?"

I smile and replied. "My favorite color is also blue." Putting my hands over my face and closing my eyes, I thought really hard for a moment. With a big sigh I said. "I want to show you something I learned when I was small. It's really neat."

I gently took the box of crayons out of his hands and started looking at all the different colors. I took each crayon I needed out, and I laid them in a row side by side.

I gave a big smile and said, "aren't you glad God created a colorful world? Color adds so much to life, just look at the beautiful fall trees. Color grabs your attention and creates moods. Color sends a message to the world around us."

The color I needed to send my message were black, red, white, blue, green, purple, and yellow. "There." I said.

Jimmy looked at me and started to laugh. "what's with all the crayons?"

I smiled and said, "This is what I learned about these special crayons."

I picked up each color in turn, and this is what I said. "The black crayon represents sin. For all have sinned and fall short of the glory of God." Romans 3: 23.

"The red represents the blood Jesus shed for us. While we were still sinners, Christ died for us. We, have now been justified by his blood." Romans 5:8-9.

"The white crayon represents forgiveness. Though your sins are like scarlet, they shall be as white as snow. We, received the cleansing of our sins." Isaiah 1:18.

"The blue crayon represents the baptism that identifies us with Jesus. No one can enter the kingdom of God unless he is born of water and the spirit." John 3: 5.

"The green represents the new life we have in Jesus. But grow in the grace and knowledge of our lord and savior Jesus Christ." 2 Peter 3:18.

"The purple crayon represents the crown of life. Be ye faithful, unto death and I will give thee the crown of life." Rev 2:10

"The yellow crayon represents eternal life. Jesus said, I am going to prepare a place for you, that you may be where I am." John 14:2-3.

Jimmy's eyes lit up as he put the crayons back in the box. He slowly closed the lid of the box and then turned towards me and said. "That was really neat. Now, I really like my crayons."

I smiled and replied. "All those color crayons were called colors of faith."

The Tree House

This time of the year we are in the midst of cooler weather and the changing colors of the leaves on the trees.

The leaves are most often colors of orange, brown, yellow, red, and purple. Some of the leaves are crisp and slowly making their way to the ground.

Then, there's the pine tree. Made of nature's pine scent green and never changes. In resemblance to God's love for us, that is our never changing God.

Most of us like to inhale and absorb the fresh, cool air on a fall day. The sun shinning bright, giving us that ray of beauty, comfort, and warmth from within.

Just recently, we were blessed with one of those days you just couldn't stay indoors. We, had this urge to get out and explore, take in nature's beauty and country fresh air.

Driving along, we saw a three-tier small square, rectangular building. It had windows on all sides of it and the siding was of distinctive colors that gave it a beautiful appearance.

It caught your attention and curiosity. One person commented, "There's a tree inside that building. Someone built a structure around a tree. "My thoughts were. "What's so important about having a tree enclosed?" I was puzzled.

Driving on, we became curious…. "Hey, getting back to the rectangular, three-tier building, why would someone enclose a tree?"

The person replied, "There was a little boy who was 12 years in age. He often said to his father, when are you going to build me a tree house? He wanted his father to build him a tree house, that was his plea, that's all he wanted from his father."

We questioned, "So, he built a building around the tree so he could play in it on a rainy day, bad weather day?"

The person said "The father only built a structure around the tree."

"One day, the little boy was biking and he got hit by a vehicle and died. The father never built the tree house, for his son's life was shortened. He did, however, build a structure around the tree. He put lights in it that pointed to the sky. The little boy can now play in his tree house, but in the tree house of heaven"

It's amazing, to hear and see how other people wrap their own heart-wrenching stories around an experience in life and redirect that story back to our creator. What a learning experience and a day of adventure all tucked and enclosed in a special design to share with others.

Do This In Remembrance Of Me

Years ago, it was very common in the home to make home-made bread. Gathering together the flour, yeast, eggs, oil, and all the necessary ingredients to make those eye appealing savory loaves of bread.

It took time to kneed the bread dough, roll it over and knead it again and again. Into the greased bread pan the bread dough went. Gently, the bread pans were covered with a towel, and patiently, the bread maker waited for the bread to rise.

Soon, the bread was ready for the oven, in a short time, the aroma of the bread baking spread throughout the home.

There is nothing more eye appealing, than a loaf of homemade bread with butter glazed over the top of it. Years ago, this was a daily routine for making homemade bread. It was somewhat of a process and routine.

It was a pleasure to share the homemade bread with family and friends! It was a delightful addition to any table gathering.

When Jesus works with Bread, He too, usually has His routine: looking to heaven, blessing, breaking and finally giving. When He gives there's always enough. Bread from Jesus will never run out, because it is His very body, given on the cross for the life of the entire world.

Another time in particular, Jesus took five loaves and two fish, He looked up into heaven and said a blessing, and broke the loaves and gave them to the disciples.

He then divided the two fish among them all. They ate until they had their fill.

They gathered up enough leftovers to fill 12 baskets, besides what remained of the fish.

Those who had eaten the loaves numbered five thousand men.

At that time in history the women and children ate, but weren't figured in the head count as they were considered properly in other words. He fed a multitude of people Matthew 15: 32-38.

Again, down the road, Jesus and His 12 disciples ate together.

The Lord's Supper, from Matthew 26:26. This time they not only ate together, Jesus gave them instructions. "Eat the bread," Jesus said. "When I am gone you will do this again and again. Then, you will think of the way I died for you."

Jesus friends ate the bread. But they were sad. They didn't want Jesus to die.

If you look around the world, nation-wide the breaking of bread is a routine. It is done in the sacrament of the Alter in remembrance for what He did for each and everyone of us.

Come to the table, not because you must, but. because you may. Come to the table, not with a hard heart, but... with an open heart. Come to the table, not because of friends and family, come and come again to... "Do this in remembrance of me."

For Unto Us A Savior Was Born

(December)

The Greatest Gift

It's that time of the year when we're all trying to look for that one special gift for our friends and loved ones.

We, search many long hours deciding what to give and how to get it comfortably and affordably. This deserves some reflection on it's own.

We, may get used to the fact that Christmas will arrive Dec. 25, weather we're ready for it or not.

Gifts in the Christmas story are not at all the gifts we would be able to find at a mall, or mail order catalog.

The angels gifts were tidings of comfort, joy, and peace. The shepherd boy's gift was generosity, his favorite lamb for the baby's birthday present.

The three kings from the east traveled many miles following a bright star in search of the birth of the baby Jesus.

The little drummer boy played his drum, for this was all he had, this was his gift. His playing brought a smile to the baby's face.

Mary delivered the greatest gift known to mankind, baby Jesus. The child brought forgiveness and saved the world from it's sins.

Gifts are made and wrapped in many different ways. Some gifts surprise and delight. Some gifts nurture the souls of both the giver and then given. Some gifts are tied with heartstrings. Some gifts are wrapped with creativity and pleasure.

The greatest gift that will ever be known throughout history at Christmas time is the fact that, "Jesus is the reason for the season." No wrapping paper, decorative bag, fancy frilly bows are needed. He fills the needs of all ages unconditionally, with no strings attached!

The Light Of The World

We, all know how it feel to be in total darkness. It can feel lonely and scary. Throughout the Bible darkness is used as a symbol of life without Jesus, and light is used as a symbol of life with Jesus.

Jesus said, "I am the light of the world. Whoever follows me will never walk in darkness, but will have the light of life." John 8:12 NIV

The world is dark with sin and unbelief. We, daily hear from bad acts of conduct or perhaps were a part of them and don't know which way to turn. Our lives, however, are enlightened because Jesus restored us to God and transformed our lives to do good.

Therefore, we are to let our light shine before others by doing good deeds. Let it be known that honorable Christians shine brightly and spread the light of Jesus to others in many forms.

How wonderful to know that with Jesus in our lives, we never have to feel alone or afraid.

One thing about the candle that we were taught was that a candle, while burning, will not lose any of its light while trying to light another candle.

This brings my thoughts to an artist who once painted a picture of a stormy and wintry twilight, and a dark, dreary house. It was a sad picture. Then, with a quick brush of yellow paint, he put a light in one window, his entire scene became one of comfort and cheer.

Being with the Christmas season, the candles we light should remind us of this. Not just the candle on the advent wreath, but even the ones in our window.

It has been told that a very poor couple living in Austria started the tradition of putting a candle in their window at Christmas. Though they had little to give, they felt blessed so they put a candle in their window to share its warm glow with people who passed by.

The other villagers wanted to know how this couple could be so happy, although so poor.

Others then followed the idea and put a candle in the window, too, to see if that was the secret.

Now, you will find in stores all around these special candles described and sold as "Welcome Candles."

To this day, the beautiful custom of placing a lighted candle in the window on Christmas is observed all over the world, sending for a message of love, hope, and cheer.

This Christmas season may we ponder this message:

The Lord is my light and my salvation. Psalm 27: 1 NIV

The Candy Cane Is Special

As, we prepare for the Christmas holiday, it's apparent that it's a very busy time of the year.

There's the cooking, cleaning, indoor and outdoor decorating, Christmas cards, church, functions, school Christmas programs, community festivities, the traditional business parties, and gift buying for loved ones.

The store ads shout the holiday sale prices at us. We, check one thing off our to-do- list and add three more.

Other than the traditional gift buying, I also started purchasing some of the fun stocking stuffer candy Items ahead of time, before they were all gone.

Searching high and low in the store, I found the special piece of candy that not only tastes good, but has a special message attached to it as well. That is the "Candy Cane."

The candy canes are special, they help us remember who Christmas is really all about.

This is a story we were taught from childhood on up, that still holds a heartwarming message within the Christmas season.

To write about the special story today, helps prevent the story from fading away from the world around us.

It all started with a candy maker from India who wanted to make a candy that would help us remember who Christmas is really about.

So, he made a Christmas candy cane. His thoughts were to incorporate several symbols for the birth, ministry and death of Jesus Christ.

He began with a stick of pure white, hard candy. Chocolate candy would have never gotten his message across as the white candy symbolized purity and the sinless nature of Jesus.

He chose a hard candy to symbolize the solid rock on which we stand, the foundation of the church, and the firmness of the promises of God.

The candy maker made the candy into the form of a, "J" to represent the name of Jesus.

The "J" would make you think of the little baby Jesus who laid in a manger and later on, would save the world from our sins. It also brings to mind the staff of the "Good Shepherd."

The candy maker then included three red stripes. This represents the suffering Christ endured at the end of His life.

Some candy canes made now, have green stripes, along with the red and white. The green symbolizes the green Christmas tree. A tree that stays green all year long, just like Jesus love for us, it never changes and lasts all year long.

The candy cane has been seen hanging on the Christmas trees, tucked inside the Christmas stockings, and freely given away at parades. It's amazing how a piece of candy, being used for a Christmas decoration, can bring out the best message to us during the Christmas season.

God Sent Us A Savior

This time of the year most of us are excited about the Christmas season.

We, search for our Christmas decorations in the attic or basement. All the boxes and totes are filled with Christmas lights, ornaments, tree stand, tree top, tree skirt, special mementos received over the years, and nativity sets.

The nativity set is completely arranged and ready for viewing, we may sense love, joy, peace, gratefulness, hope, and fulfillment within ourselves.

Sometimes we may wonder, If God would have done things differently, how or what would our world be like?

If, our greatest need would have been for someone to figure out the world step-by step or inch by inch with a tape measure, God would have sent a mathematician, but he didn't.

If, our greatest need would have been for someone to gather information, teach, and inform others, God would have sent us an educator, but he didn't.

If, our greatest need would have been laptops, computers, or extended technology, God would have sent us a scientist, but he didn't.

If, our greatest need would have been money, gold, silver, or lavish wealth driven with power, God would have sent us an economist, but he didn't.

If, our greatest need would have been pleasure trips, cruise ships, jet skies, motorcycles, limos, carriage rides, or sports cars, God would have sent us an entertainer, but he didn't.

Our greatest need was humbly simplified, for each and every one of us. It took a tree that was once was rooted to become the wooden cross. It took three nails to hold him to the cross and a crown of thorns to prove to us, that he had complete his work in the world. Our greatest need was forgiveness so God sent us a Savior.

God didn't send baby Jesus to a throne to live beyond his means, but to a manger filled with hay.

Jesus lived not as a prince or a king, but as a servant. My king didn't come here to be served. He came here to serve others with his feet, hands, and voice.

Jesus chose not to be selfish or self-centered. He gave just a little but everything, just for the love of us.

Sending A Message Of Love, Hope, And Cheer

One night, when coming home from work, I was admiring at a distance our Christmas tree all lit up, lights of every color beautifully displayed through our patio glass doors.

When seeing all the different lights, it gave me a feeling of peace and calmness.

Then, on our picnic table (so it won't get covered in deep snow) we have Rudolf and a sleigh covered in lights. Of course, Santa is standing in the midst, covered in lights, as jolly and happy as can be.

It gave me a feeling of excitement and happiness.

In my kitchen window, we placed a single candle that is lit up. It stands all alone by itself. We, all know how it feels to be in total darkness. It can feel lonely and scary.

Throughout the Bible, darkness was used as a symbol of life without Jesus, and light is used as a symbol of life with Jesus.

While growing up, I learned a story about a very poor couple living in Austria, who started the tradition of putting a candle in their window at Christmas. Though, they had little to give, they felt blessed, so they put a candle in their window to share is warm glow with people who passed by.

The other villagers wanted to know how this couple could be so happy, although so poor.

Others then followed their idea and put a candle in their window, too, to see if that was the secret.

To this day, the beautiful custom of placing a lighted cand the window on Christmas is observed all over the world, sending forth a message of love, hope, and cheer.

The Christmas season we ponder this message. "The Lord is my light and my salvation." Psalm 27:1 NIV

About The Author

Pam Fiecke's former English Teacher communicates to all, the fine details of a creative writing journey, that has finally come to a wrap-up for all to enjoy!

I, Mr. Robert Henning taught English in Lester Prairie High School for 35 years. Even in Pam's junior high years, her creative writing talent was very evident. She quickly learned the fundamentals, and then advanced her style and word choice to make her writing interesting and meaningful. Her love for writing grew as her talent "blossomed."

When I would give her one and two page assignments, she would enthusiastically turn in five or more pages. She was an excellent learner, always willing to put forth the extra effort to create memorable writings. Her description was clear and effective, and her characters were interesting. Her word choice was fresh and vital, always drawing the reader toward a meaningful conclusion. Pam did excellent work.

Pam's creative writing work under my supervision, culminated with the publication of her first novel within the onset of High School Graduation. (Yesterday's Tears Becomes Tomorrows Smiles.) I, was—and remain proud of her. I, welcome Pam's first edition, (Inspirational Stories that Spark Our Emotions and Touch the Heart and Soul) also, receiving the Platinum Seal. Now, her second edition, (Memories are a Reflection of our Past) is on the "Must Read" list. Her many year journey from my Creative Writing classroom to these two new books, has been interrupted, but never abandoned. Her Inspirational Stories are positive, hopeful, and uplifting-desirable and valuable reading in today's troubled world. Pam has a strong work-ethic, and an optimistic personality. Her love for writing, and her unwavering faith in the irrepressible human spirit have lured her into sharing these stories with us. Her words-without being cutesy or peachy-evoke warm smiles, and gently remind us that being positive and hopeful are necessary keys to achieving happy lives.

Robert D. Henning (Hutchinson, MN)
Instructor of English, Retired
Lester Prairie Public School, MN

About The Author

Pam and I have been friends since the age of 13. She values faith, family, and friendship, community, and much more.

Her values show in her writings. When Pam sits down to write, it seems like the words flow easily, from her mind to the paper and comes together smoothly.

For a small-town women, living in the Midwest, she has blossomed herself through many forms of writing. Bless her heart for sharing her gift of creative writings, which give pleasure, inspire, and comfort, the many people she touches through her words.

Linda Giesen
Friend
Waverly, MN

About The Author

My long time friend, Pam Fiecke, writes beautifully and from her heart always.

Her Inspirational Stories are very touching and uplifting for anyone dealing with grief, adult sadness, or anxiety. Her writings reflect her very caring soul for her family, friends, and community.

Diane Gustad
Friend
Winsted, MN

About The Author

The Herald-Journal of Winsted, MN. Express their thoughts of Pam Fiecke's column, "Inspirational Thoughts," and writing career.

"Pam Fiecke is a thoughtful writer who has attracted a loyal audience. She is persistent, reliable and inspiring."

Chris Schultz
CEO/ Publisher
Herald Journal Newspaper
Friend
Lester Prairie, MN

About The Author

Pam is a wonderful person, very outgoing, kind, and overflowing with joy. Her writings are very Inspirational, down to earth, easy to read, and brightens your day.

Sue Dressel
Friend
Waconia, MN

About The Author

For anyone seeking a genuinely heartfelt and up lifting reading experience, I wholeheartedly recommend Pam Fiecke's books, especially, "Inspirational Stories That Spark Our Emotions And Touch The Heart And Soul," first edition, and now, her second edition, "Memories Are A Reflection Of Our Past."

Pam has a remarkable gift for weaving narratives that resonate deeply, drawing on her strong faith and genuine connection to community. Her writing is not just about telling stories, it's about sharing wisdom, offering comfort, and encouraging a positive outlook on life. If you're looking for words that will inspire you, touch your heart, and leave you feeling more hopeful, you'll find a true treasure in her work. Its clear, her books come from a place of deep care and a desire to uplift every reader.

Andrew Meuleners
General Manager/ Herald Journal
Publishing/ Newspaper
Friend
Winsted, MN

About The Author

Pam Fiecke is a talented and compassionate storyteller, gifted with the ability to craft narratives that resonate deeply with the readers. With a passion that shines through in every word, it inspires and uplifts through her work, leaving a lasting impact on all who read her stories. As creative force to be reckoned with, continues to weave magic with words, touching hearts and minds alike.

Blake Shelton
Friend
Oklahoma

About The Author

Pam's Inspirations for her books, attribute form her community projects, she does around the small community of Winsted, MN. Her first edition book, "Inspirational Stories that Spark our Emotions and Touch the Heart and Soul," receiving the Platinum Seal from Citi of Books, Albuquerque, NM, in a short time. Now, the second edition book, "Memories are a Reflection of our Past," is on the must read list of things to do! The stories are easy to read and add much to the heart and soul.

Sarah Franke
Friend
Texas

About The Author

Pam is a very extremely dedicated and motivated woman who has worked hard to hone her craft.

She always carries a smile, and oftentimes it spreads to those around her.

Her writing speaks for itself while also speaking to others, as she uses her real-world experiences to connect to readers in a deep, meaningful way.

Austen Neaton
Herald Journal/
Staff Writer/Sports
Friend
Watertown, MN

About The Author

Pam has provided "Inspirational Thoughts" in a column, to our local area newspapers for many years and now expanded her reach with the success of her first edition, "Inspirational Stories that Spark our Emotions and Touch the Heart and Soul" and now, her second edition, "Memories are a Reflection of our Past."

Dan Birkholz

Friend

Digital & Production Manager

at the Herald Journal Winsted

About the Author

It's a thrill to see someone of our own, Pam Fiecke, having success with her books, and best of all that her Inspirational stories point us to Jesus Christ, the Savior who died for us and promises eternal life for all who believe.

Dale Kovar
Friend
General Manager at the
Herald Journal Publishing — Winsted
(Author of Joseph Wore Tennis Shoes:
Stories From Small Town Journalism)

About the Author

I have worked with Pam for many years on some of the many community activities that Pam participates in. She has boundless energy for many activities. She has a true passion for community service. Anyone who attends any of her events can immediately tell she is in her element. The whole community benefits from Pam as a resident.

Jason Blashack
Herald Journal Sales Rep.
Friend
Lester Prairie, MN

My Autobiography

Just as I was, a child heading off to school like any other insecure child, scared, who am I going to know, my stomach was turning, the school bus was big and colored orange and spacious, and I wanted my mom and my puppy!

I attended a parochial school system at elementary level, that is where I accumulated my strong religious evangelism background. In school, on a day to day basis, I was loved, encouraged, taught about Jesus, and built-up like every other student, to have faith and live that faith anchored and armored by the word of God. We, were taught morals, values, integrity, evangelism and religion in a very concrete way. We, lived out our teachings and became a great example to others. In great sadness our parochial school closed, leaving us with no other option but to the public school system. I loved writing, it traveled with me. A piece of paper laid before me and a #2 pencil in my hand. I learned the fundamentals, creative writing 1, creative writing 2, then, excelled to advanced creative writing. Before Graduating from high school, I mastered being an Author of my first Published book by the age of 18. "Yesterday's Tears Become Tomorrows Smiles."

My teacher commended me for excellence in the writing field. Following high school, I continued writing, never abandoning myself from writing, however, I kept myself silent to the public. I took aptitude tests for writing children's books, with returned excellent results. I was in a Writers Guild Training Session, my discovery was, my skills were equal to those of the Professional Authors.

I, ventured into learning and have a successful background in business, sales and service with Home Interiors and Gifts. I was taught many positive tools for success and at the same time I was inspired by the direction and steps I had learned while in business.

This led me to having learned different strengths and living a healthy and productive lifestyle as a woman.

In 2004, I was selected as Hometown Hero for my community of Winsted for outstanding service. I, have successfully ran organized and volunteered with many functions over the years.

In 2005, the Herald Journal Newspaper, Chris Schultz, CEO/Publisher and Dale Kovar, General mgr. Phoned me, met with me and handed me a column to continue my Inspirational Stories. Now, I was going to be a columnist! I, named my column "Inspirational Thoughts," this is where my writing blossomed and my light was shown more evident!

On my journey, I decided to expand my religious beliefs and become a Sunday School Teacher, for Holy Trinity Church, followed by, in time became the coordinator of the program for 21 years. This was a good experience for me and our four children!

In 2006, I, decided not only to be a columnist but, I wanted to write Momentous writings for the deceased. I, would write an Inspirational writing and personalize it with their name and the deceased date framed to set up at a wake or funeral. I put a lit candle and flowers or greenery tucked in front of the framed Inspirational writing. This is a gift to the family in behalf of their loved one.

I started having my work Copy Written through Direct Legal and my work is now in the Library of Congress.

My son, Brandon and I, participated in Missionary work in a group setting in Jamacia. It was a true experience to see what needs to be done to help others less fortunate than ourselves.

I, worked in manufacturing at Sterner Lighting in Winsted, MN for 19 ½ years assembling light fixtures, along with being on a Safety Committee.

They closed their doors permanently.

I, then headed to Crown College in Hutchinson, MN to the State of Minnesota Nursing Assistant Registry and became Registered in 2009. I, have been in Health Care/Activities ever since.

In 2011, I wrote, framed, and had copy written, for Fr. Anthony Hesse, "Forever you will be my parents." That Fr. Tony signed and gave to his parents for their Anniversary.

They loved it!

In 2012, our town of Winsted was celebrating their 125th Anniversary. I wrote a beautiful writing and presented it to the city of Winsted in behalf of their 1250) Anniversary! The writing at that time was set on a shelf in the entry for anyone to read when they came into the city building.

In great surprise, in 2012, HILLTOP Records. Found one of my writings in the Library of Congress in Washington D.C. Over a million people have their work in this building. To me, it was like finding a needle in a haystack!

I, gave them one song to put music too and decided to go with Paramount of Nashville who also contracted some of my lyrics! Paramount did beautiful work with my lyrics songs!

KDUZ in Hutchinson did interviews with me and played my songs as well!

My lyrics songs were on C.D.'s and received a Gold Award for "A Halo and a Set of Golden Wings."

In 2013, Paramount wanted to put some of my songs on a C.D. called, "Catch a Rising Star,"

In 2016, T decided to start family Bingo, Chicken Bingo, in the fall time and Fishing with the Bunny, in spring time. We, have two groups to man handle each event, with one being non-profit with the 501C. This includes, 13 games of Bingo, Concessions, Silent Action, Dollar Raffle, Live Auction, Door Prizes, and the event is themed! A Chicken or a Bunny will do a nice "Welcome" to music and hand out treats to those Bingo players!

An absolutely fun time for all involved!! The two businesses who help out receive the profit for whatever they need money for, to help them along the way!

I continually, help with the Festival Parade, where my husband, Steve and I, received in 2024, the Honorary Commodore Award! We, were chosen for, recognition of dedicated volunteer service and community Involvement for the city of Winsted!

We, continue volunteering with the church, Winstock Country Music and where- ever needed to help out!

In the writing field, I am still active in being a columnist with the Herald Journal for 20 years and will continue!

I still do Momentous Writings for Funerals of people who I am close too. I, have my own stand to put my beautiful work on, at the Chilson's Funeral Home in Winsted.

I, am a country music lyricist and have C.D.'s and other prominent lead musicians interested in my lyrics work as I write!!

I, have been an Author right out of High School and have been on a solid journey for over 47 years!

In 2024, I received the Platinum Seal for my Inspirational Book, "Inspirational Stories that Spark our Emotions and Touch the Heart and Soul."

At the largest Librarian event in the USA, out of 156 books, 10 Directors selected three books that were outstanding in all areas of their book, and my Inspirational Book was one of them that was selected!! "Inspirational Stories that Spark Our Emotions and Touch the Heart and Soul."

All three of us selected, then ventured onto being put on a 17 by 8 ft. digital billboard in Albuquerque, NM for a period of time!

I, have written three books to date, "Yesterday's Tears becomes Tomorrows Smiles." (Right out of High School) "Inspirational Stories that Spark Our Emotions and Touch the Heart and Soul." with a platinum Seal, and newly released, second edition, "Memories are a Reflection of your Past."

All of my Inspirational reading material, brings a message to us in a healthy way and positive manner. All of the short stories will touch your heart and your soul! The books are written to bring joy and happiness to your reading adventure!

____

Author's Signature